C.S. Boag is a former journalist who has also grown potatoes, driven taxis and bulldozers and worked in a hamburger bar. He has travelled many times throughout Australia and to France, speaking enough French not to die there. He was a Sydney City Councillor for six years and holds degrees from NSW and Sydney universities as well as postgraduate qualifications from Macquarie. Besides publishing short stories he has also worked as a columnist for *Woman's Day* and the *Bulletin*. He won the Walter Stone Memorial Prize for Literature in 1986. C.S. Boag lives on a small 'green' holding near Bathurst, NSW, with his wife, Judith. He has five children.

www.csboag.com

By the same author

The Case of the Hood With No Hands

The Case of the Death of a Ladies' Man

The Case of the Horses for Corpses

The Case of the Bullets at the Ballet

The Case of the Cock Robin Killer

C.S. Boag

MISTER RAINBOW

in the Case of the

MORGUE THE MERRIER

XOUM PUBLISHING

Sydney

 XOUM

First published by Xoum in 2015

Xoum Publishing
PO Box Q324, QVB Post Office,
NSW 1230, Australia
www.xoum.com.au

ISBN 978-1-921134-69-2 (digital)
ISBN 978-1-921134-68-5 (print)

Cataloguing-in-publication data is available from the
National Library of Australia

Word count 45,000

For Alan Mills – writer, guide, friend

He was an – an – extremist.
Heart of Darkness, Joseph Conrad

Chapter 1

THE KID

He's tall and bony and he's hopping about the Camellia pier like he's high-stepping over hot sand in a Bondi heatwave. He's wearing long socks, sandals and a carnation-coloured T-shirt with a horseman swinging a polo mallet on its left bo-diddly – the kind of outfit jokers wear when they believe everything the fashionistas tell them – and the legs below his Great White Hunter shorts are matchsticks.

He called while I was minding my own business. My own business being non-existent at the time I agreed to meet him.

'It's like they're *stalking* me, you know?' he says.

'No, I don't know. But why don't you take time out from your tap dancing to tell me.'

He raises his peepers from his iPhone.

'I was attacked by a bunch of thugs but was rescued by these men who asked if I was *disaffected* with Western society. When I said *yes* – remember, I'd just been attacked – they said if I wanted to do something about it they could provide the necessary arms, ammunition and training.'

'Where?'

He ducks his head to his iPhone.

'At a camp in a secret location on the outskirts of Sydney.'

'I mean where did the incident occur?'

'Near home.'

'Where's home?'

'Vaucluse.'

A market garden for growing money.

It was late at night and he was alone. Four kids stepped out of the cover of darkness and demanded his wallet and anything else of value. When he refused they attacked him.

'Why call me?' I say.

'You came highly recommended.'

'By whom?'

He makes the kind of gesture rich men's sons make when conversations aren't going their way.

'Oh, you know, by heaps of people – I don't remember *who*.'

'Describe them.'

'How can I when I don't remember them?'

'I'm talking about the jokers that tried to recruit you.'

'Oh. They were of Middle Eastern appearance – the kind you avoid on a dark night.'

'Why would you avoid them just because they looked different?'

'It was more than that.'

It's like extracting bullets from the victim of a shooting – you got to probe and there's a lot of blood and afterwards you think it might have been better to leave the slugs where they were.

'Okay. What's your name?'

'Bertie – Bertie Thomas.'

'Bertie, let me tell you something. It's like I asked you to describe a bunch of nuns and you said they were *devout*; or that a group of boy scouts were *small, pimply-faced and helpful*. Your words don't ring true. *Of Middle Eastern appearance?* Give me a break. Next you'll be saying they were bearded and their heads were wrapped in tea towels.'

'But they were!'

I glance at the yachts bobbing about on the Harbour; you don't have to be bright to live in a place like this, just greedy. I look back at bright-eyes.

'I can't see the problem,' I say.

'I said *no*.'

'I still can't see the problem.'

He shakes his head. 'Come on, mister, people have known about this for years. If it's not al-Queda, it's Hamas, Hezbollah or the Islamic Jihad. These people are terrorists preying on disaffected kids. When I said *no* they felt vulnerable. They threatened me. I've no doubt they'll make good on their threats. I want you to frighten them off.'

'Why not go to Daddy or the police?'

The kid consults his iPhone. It's getting to be a habit.

'Before I said *no* I went to one of their meetings.' He looks up. 'Which makes me involved, too, doesn't it? I'll be on the books of the security agencies, my phone will be tapped, Daddy will find out and my life will be hell.' He sees me contemplating the expensive boats and the even more expensive houses. 'My father's not the kind of person who'd be happy having a terrorist for a son. So, yes, I need help. And don't worry, I haven't spoken to anyone else.'

I hunch my shoulders; he's given me the dough-ray-me; I suppose I need to go through the motions of earning it.

'Describe the meeting.'

'They showed us a movie called *Unbeloved Infidel*. It was blatant anti-Western propaganda with scantily-clad women flaunting themselves, men staggering around drunk and a lot of people getting up to no good. It ended with an explosion in which people were killed. When the lights came up, one of the men said they were recruiting for ISIL – he spelled out what the letters stood for. He said we could fight either here or overseas.'

'Where did this occur?'

'In some kind of hall. I don't know where it was because we were blindfolded.'

'Where did your journey start and how long did it take?'

'They picked me up near home –' he hesitates '– and the drive took an hour ...'

I keep the questions coming like I'm a one-man firing squad and the kid's got his back to the wall.

'You said *we* – how many were there?'

'About six jihadists and the same number of recruits.'

'What do the letters ISIL stand for?'

When Bertie glances down again, the eye movement's barely perceptible.

'Islamic State.'

I knock his iPhone into the water.

'There are four letters in ISIL – you only accounted for two.'

'Islamic State, Islamic Land.'

He's lost his memory or I just lost it for him.

'Try *Islamic State of Iraq and the Levant*.'

He looks like he's about to cry.

'Are you saying you don't want to take the case?'

I finger the nice, big, crisp lettuce leaves he brought me all the way from Vaucluse where they grow them.

'Bertie, I wouldn't not take this case for quids.'

Chapter 2

THE SMILEY MAN

The search engine in the computer café coughs up *Thomas, Bertie – student*, then the name of his father, which is different to his but that doesn't prove dishwater. The addresses tally and although the kid's story's far-fetched I can't see any reason why he'd lie.

Farewell to old England for-eh-eh-vah
Farewell to my rum coes as well
Farewell to the well-known Old Bay-ee-ly
Where I used for to cut such a swell.

We're in my old school gym, the curtains are purple and – to the background of the convict song containing too many incomprehensible words – the latest generation of kids is milling among control-freak teachers, bemused parents and assorted ex-students. *It's really indigo,* Rube murmurs, *the colour of memory.* The Principal is at the front of the stage, people find their seats and a kid with a mouth organ gets in one last squeak before fading into silence.

'This isn't the real thing,' the Principal says. 'But the children need to rehearse before a live audience. We'll be staging the play proper on the Friday following the Australia Day weekend. I do hope you'll all be able to make it. In the meantime – enjoy.' She claps, sits and the kids try the next lot of incomprehensible words:

Singing too-rah-li, oo-rah-li, addity,
Singing too-rah-li, oo-rah-li, ay.
Singing too-rah-li, oo-rah-li, addity,
For we're bou-ound for Bo-tan-ee Bay.

The curtain rises on a rabble of undersized convicts straggling across a stage strewn with papier-mâché rocks, lugging picks filched from Dad's garden to a backdrop of gumtrees, complete with koalas.

'Speaking of colour,' I murmur, 'it looks like we've finally grown up as a society. Those kids are from every conceivable background – a couple of them are even wearing burqas.'

'They're *hijabs*, Rainbow,' Aunt Rube says. 'Plus there's a shayla and maybe an al-amira or two. Not that it's important because we can only call ourselves civilised when we start judging people on who they are instead of what they wear. People aren't Australian, American, African, Asian, Jewish or of Middle Eastern appearance, they're people.'

Aunt Rube can be about as comfortable as a bunch of burrs in your Y-fronts. I scan the audience and a face leaps into high relief – that of a small man, smiling. He waves and I dredge my memory. But all I remember are hours in dark cupboards, getting beaten, being tied to active ant hills and suchlike. I don't recall any small, cheery kid. Beside me Rube winces. It's either the quality of the acting or her kidney.

'I'd better get you home, Rube.'

She shakes her head. 'You heard what the dame said – shut up and enjoy.'

So I shut up and what I see is a bunch of kids acting out Australian history the way too many people imagine it happened – a nice Captain Cook claiming an unoccupied land in the name of a distant King; a couple of fine Governors; intrepid explorers; Rum Corps soldiers swigging cold tea out of Coke bottles; awed Aborigines; and a lot of hard-working white men. Now and then one of the convicts waves to his parents.

When it all goes up in smoke I'm down on the floor with my gat out in a nanosecond. Vapour fills the air, lights flash and chain-gangers tumble left, right and centre. Over the top of the commotion a voice booms: *To forge a way across the Blue Mountains, workers used dynamite. Casualties were many but work that was vital to the opening up of the Western Plains continued until …*

I take in the crowd. The smiley man's still there. So, too, is a shadow that might be Pandora, the nemesis that's been after me for as long as I can remember.

'Get up off the floor, Rainbow – it's only a stage effect,' Rube murmurs. 'Remember our lessons on explosives?'

I put away the gat and climb back into my seat. Yeah, I remember. Aunt Rube taught me how to handle live rockets, defuse time bombs and disable detonators – we even dabbled in nuclear technology.

'I haven't forgotten a thing you taught me, Rube.'

'Notice everything's *terrorism* these days? It's like those little faces they call – what is it: *motor-cons ...*'

Me and Harry go back to when he was a bookie with his life in front of him, long before he got into the brawl with the crooked gamblers that persuaded him to retire to this hole-in-the-wall caff in Cammeray. We got no secrets from each other, me and Harry. He even once showed me his distinguishing marks – in case he copped it and needed to be ID'd. *You won't get killed, Harry,* I assured him but he shook his head. *Everyone cops it one way or another, Rain.*

'It's emoticons.'

'That's what I said – those things that save people thinking. Like words such as *terrorism* that people use as shorthand for *Don't Trust Anyone.* The way that the letters *L.O.L.* stand for *Little Old Lady.*'

'It's *Laugh Out Loud*, Harry.'

But Harry's on a roll.

'Terrorism means different things to different people. To politicians it's votes; to some, it's an outlet for their insecurity; to others, it's a man in a balaclava doing a beheading. Know what I mean?'

Chapter 3

INSIDE THE BLUE BALLOON

'No, what *do* you mean, Harry?'

'I mean that everyone has the potential be a terrorist – whether they're husband, wife, sister, brother or just someone that pushes past you too hard in the street.'

He goes back in his hole-in-the-wall caff while I flap the wrinkles out of the newspaper. Sometimes it's hard getting things straight at Harry's. The table wobbled when I arrived so I propped up one of its legs with a serviette only to find the same problem with another leg so I levelled it with a bottle top but that only made matters worse. Take that caper far enough and you end up with a stairway to heaven, to discover when you get there that the table still wobbles.

'Hey, Harry!'

He emerges looking like he's been mauled by a pack of dingoes. 'What?'

'Ever consider getting three-legged tables?'

'Why?'

'Because it's a scientifically proven fact that you can't level four-legged ones. Ever hear of the sixth law of dynamics?'

He frowns, suspecting a trick.

'Maybe.'

'Then you heard it too late. Science has moved on since Einstein. Now it's the Convergence of Unrelated Phenomena – or *COUP*, for short.'

'You been drinking, Rainbow?'

'No, I've been reading the *Daily Terrorgraph* which is the next best thing. It's the usual blood-letting: an editorial on how our society's obsessed with sex – with a photo of a near-naked dame on the front page to prove it; a totally unrelated story about the convergence of unrelated phenomena; all wrapped up in a piece saying that our Australia Day spectacular will be, well, spectacular.'

'In my humble opinion, Rainbow, the *Terrorgraph* presents a greatly oversimplified view of things.'

I start on my burnt mushrooms.

'There's nothing simple about the convergence of unrelated phenomena, Harry.'

'So explain.'

I take a stab at the toast but it rejects the knife, the table wobbles again and the newspaper slides to the ground.

'It goes something like: *While one action doesn't necessarily follow another, in the end it probably does. Which doesn't mean that things that seem totally unrelated aren't.*'

'Aren't what?'

'Totally unrelated.'

Harry drags out a seat and sits down like everything's suddenly got too much for him.

'I'm glad you explained that, Rainbow.'

It's one of those days when a clear sky arches over the city like a blue balloon and shadows exist where they shouldn't. Maybe it's the table, maybe it's Harry, maybe it's the newspaper, but more than likely it's the totally unrelated convergence of all three.

Harry leans forward.

'Some bastard broke my window.'

'Who?'

He shrugs.

'Either a gang, a window-fixing company or a bunch of those terrorists we were talking about.'

That's when Tsunami shows up and asks what we're eating.

I'd told Tsunami – that's Sue Mahoney, pronounced Sue *Mah-nee*, hence the moniker – that we might catch up one day, meaning never. And to prove that I meant what I said when I didn't, I wrote Aunt Rube's address on one of Harry's table napkins, which Tsunami immediately attached to her scooter. So what does she do after that? She turns up at Harry's for breakfast. Which today consists of Harry's undrinkable coffee, a couple of rounds of toast carefully burnt around the edges, and coagulated sugar in a bowl the size and weight of an eight-inch cannonball.

They're on the other side of the road dismantling a bus stop, five of them – male, clean-cut and young.

I turn to Harry.

'Are those thugs over there somehow connected to you?'

He indicates the broken window. 'They're the ones that did that. They must be waiting for you to leave.'

Harry's wrong on one count – they're not waiting for us to leave. Because they're already crossing the road, shoving each other around and shouting on the approach. They're wearing a kind of uniform – red T-shirts teamed with leather jackets, jeans and lace-up boots.

'Why?'

Harry shakes his head as if to clear it.

'I must have upset them somehow.'

'Describe the *somehow.*'

'I got the scimitar that I keep behind the counter and told them if they didn't clear out I'd dice them and serve them for dinner.'

I turn my attention back to the gang.

'That'd do it.'

Chapter 4

A DANGEROUS MISTRESS

'What did you learn tonight, Rainbow?' Rube asks as I walk her home after the rehearsal. As we pass the old Darlinghurt Jail I hear the clanking of the treadmill, the stretching of the rack and the moaning of the wind where the gallows used to be. I learnt: *Don't expect nothing from nobody and you'll never be disappointed.* But I don't tell Rube that.

'What do you mean, Rube?'

'Come on, I know you like I know Rumsford's *Rules of Evidence.* Something's got to you.'

I tell her about the terrorist case I'm on – courtesy of Bertie – and I feel her glance at me.

'That's a coincidence because I'm looking into terrorism, too.' She frowns. 'Be careful. Certain people don't like my being involved. There have been threats. And if you're not careful, you might come under sway of the same logic.'

'What's the nature of the threats?'

'Death threats to me personally – using my name, on my computer, in notes and by way of graffiti – calling me an *infidel pig* and saying I'll die in the name of Allah.'

'Jesus, Rube, why didn't you tell me this before?'

She shrugs. 'Because I knew you'd get hot under the collar, Rainbow, just as you're doing now. Come on, private eyes get threats all the time – you of all people should know that.'

'What did you mean about *indigo* being the colour of memory?'

'The word's been on my mind. Life's like being lowered into a bottomless pit. In the first flush of youth you have all the hot colours – the reds, oranges and pinks. But as you grow older and the pit gets deeper, you get your greens and blues – what I call the *shadow colours*. Until in your twilight years everything's indigo. Are you listening to me, Rainbow?'

Maybe I am and maybe I'm distracted by the shadow by the old jail that could be Pandora because it's too substantial to be a wraith and too ever-present to be coincidental. The lights of a passing car cut a swath through the mist while from the Harbour comes the echoing boom of a foghorn.

'Yeah, I'm listening. And what I'm hearing is a lot of death talk.'

'What if it is? People like me don't live forever. I'm a private detective – long and happy retirements are for others.'

The thugs are still coming our way.

'These people don't look like your regular clientele, Harry.'

Under his nine o'clock shadow Harry's become a whiter shade of pale.

'I haven't *got* a regular clientele, Rain. After a long and generally unhappy life I find myself with few compensations apart from this place. I'm alone and as far as possible I'd like to keep it that way. Consequently, I do my best to repel boarders.'

Drivers are afraid to go forwards or backwards in case they hit one of the mincemeats and get sued for it. I count four of the thugs before looking away. Which is when I spot the fifth – busy examining Tsunami's scooter like it's a species of cockroach. Even as I watch, he takes something off it before kicking the bike into the gutter. It's like a signal – his cronies leave off their game with the cars and start towards us at a trot.

Harry slips into the chair next to Tsunami – like getting up close and personal to an ex-marine might make for greater security – but Tsunami immediately shifts away from him. She also picks up the cannon-ball sugar bowl. I get out of her line of fire. The writing on the nearside arm of the lead boy says:

TEROR 4 EVA

Five sets of shoulders hunch and I read their intentions as easy as I can read the words on the kid's arm but without the spelling errors. Tsunami brings back her arm like she's waving.

Cheap sugar dispensers are heavy and this one's no exception. It arcs through the air and hits one kid and the shrapnel takes out the boy next door. I roll from my chair and take out the next two in the assembly line with what I call my *Nutcracker*

Sweet: smacking a couple of heads together before grinding them like dried berries in a pepper mill with the setting on *COARSE*. Which leaves one thug standing – easy pickings and we pick him.

Harry tenses for the follow-through but there isn't one. The thugs break camp, helping each other off the canvas and back into the bleachers while a stray dog fossicks for scraps. I set my chair back on its feet.

'It looks like we need another breakfast, Harry.'

'Thanks for that,' Harry says as he brings out more burnt toast and more undrinkable coffee.

I dust off my hands. It's only a gesture – I hardly got them dirty.

'Don't mention it.'

Harry shakes his head. 'Irony's too subtle for you, Rainbow. I wasn't thanking you in the traditional sense. In plain English, you and your girlfriend have just put the *UNDER NEW MANAGEMENT* sign up on my caff.' He nods towards the retreating gang. 'Jokers like that see resistance as a gilt-embossed invitation on which the letters *R.S.V.P.* stand for *Really Severe Vengeance Proposed*.'

I feel sorry for Harry but *sorry* doesn't buy nobody a suit of body armour so me and Tsunami clean up while Harry telephones the glass people. Going by the wait they're starting from scratch.

'Have you dealt with this lot before?'

'The thugs?'

'No, the glass people.'

Harry shakes his head. 'This is the first time. The old ones folded — they couldn't handle the transparency-in-business laws.'

The glass people arrive in one of those tent-backed trucks they use for carting glass around in, *A GLASS ACT: all pane, no pain* written along the side. They lift the glass into place with suction cups and slap their sticker in the bottom left-hand corner so they can be called when it happens again. By which time I'm no longer paying attention. Which is why me and Tsunami head off into the sunset together aboard Tsunami's scooter.

'Where are you going?' I call through my visor.

'Where you're going.'

'I'm going home.'

'Where's home?'

'The boat.'

I steady the dinghy as she climbs aboard, a sassy, hourglass shape in figure-hugging black easing herself onto the wraparound deck of the *Wooden No* (*What's your boat called?* Nosey Parkers ask, to which I reply: *Wooden No*). Once we're aboard, I get my half-hitch in a knot and by the time I reach the stateroom she's found the Glenlivet and when she hands me my jar her fingers are electric eels fresh off the charger.

Time for a cautionary shot across the bows.

'Loneliness is a dangerous mistress, Tsunami.' I

could be warning myself. 'Which is why you got to drown your misapprehensions before they grow into cats and scratch your eyes out. After which I'll row you ashore and you can go home.'

Without waiting for a response I make my way down to the bilge. Starting the pump isn't just to keep the boat afloat – it's to keep my head above water as well. I hear a sound like thunder and to distract myself I murmur: *Remember the engine oil.* Because in the Case of the Cock Robin Killer, Skinny Minnie destroyed the pump by forgetting the oil.

Chapter 5

NOT EVEN CLOSE

When I get back to the stateroom I find the cause of the thunder. Tsunami's dragged the mattresses out of the cabins and lashed them together and now she's busy covering them with canvas. I stay by the hatch, a place of relative safety.

'Let's go,' I say.

'Where are we going?'

'It's not where *we're* going, Tsunami, it's where *you're* going – back to your home in Balmain.'

'Oh, really?'

It starts bad and ends worse. Tsunami tries to get drunk and fails. Then she takes off all her clothes and lies down, patting the mattress beside her and inviting me to join her. When I refuse – saying what she's got in mind is the worst idea since the invention of money – she gets upset. After which she falls asleep, leaving me to consider her scars.

About midnight, she opens her eyes. I look up

from the scars.

'What happened?'

She takes a deep breath. 'They're war wounds. A bit of shrapnel and I was knifed once. That one's my appendectomy.'

'I'm talking about the other scar – the one that no-one can see.'

She looks away.

'Enemies can be anything from bona fide soldiers to kids armed with rocket launchers and axes – some even used forks and bottle openers out of the knife drawer in the kitchen. Wars aren't parlour games, Rainbow. After I was taken prisoner, my captors behaved in the way captors have behaved since time began. And since then I –'

I don't say anything. It's not deliberate. I don't know what to say.

'It doesn't matter,' I tell her at last.

'What *does* matter then?' Her voice is bitter – she's staring at the shadows criss-crossing the ceiling. 'Does Harry matter? Your Aunt Rube? Your daughter? Do *you* matter for that matter? Does *anyone*?' She shakes her head. 'You think I'm selfish, that there are a lot of people worse off than me – that the inability to be intimate isn't the end of the world.'

She moves away the way she distanced herself from Harry – all that's missing is the sugar bowl. Not because she wants to but because she can't help herself and when she speaks again she's talking to spectres.

'You knew I couldn't bear Harry being close to me and would have guessed it wasn't just him.

That's why I was a successful soldier and also why I chucked the sugar bowl as hard as I did, nearly killing that kid in the process. I translate my fear into violence just like those kids do. Do you know what was done to me?'

'I can guess.'

She shakes her head.

'You wouldn't even come close.'

Because of the darkness, I know where the water is only by its resistance to the oars. A vessel black as Fate passes, making me pause in my rowing. But as soon as the water settles I start up again and when I beach the coracle, Tsunami's reluctant to disembark, like she thinks she might be stepping onto quicksand.

'You should have let me face my devils, Rainbow. I know I can beat them. Can't we at least give it a go?'

I shake my head in the darkness. 'Imagine yourself on a permanent war footing, Tsunami, and you'd have some idea what it would be like being with me.' I remember Rube and the threats. 'A private eye never knows if he'll see tomorrow.'

She's lost the ability to feel, she says. After growing up at the mercy of a born-to-kill brother, the Army offered a chance to escape. At first it worked – being a soldier seemed to enable her to feel again. But in the end it only made matters worse.

I try to reassure her.

'It's not just *you* that life doesn't fit, Tsunami.

Existence isn't made to measure – life's the hand you're dealt; it's off the hook, one size fits all.' I think of Imogene. 'Apart from which, attachments make people vulnerable.'

A weariness overcomes her. She climbs out of the boat, clambers across the rocks and scrambles through the trees to her bike. I hear the little motor putt-putt to life as I get the coracle back in the water. The echo of my reply keeps time with the oars as I row back to the hulk, as if rebounding from the walls of a labyrinth: *vulnerable, vulnerable, vulnerable …*

Early the following morning a mobile rings – one of the unsafe ones. I pick up but don't answer.

'That you, Rainbow?'

I don't exist – I got no property, no bank account, no Medicare number, no email, no licence of any kind and no name to speak of. Which makes me no more than a careless word on an unguarded phone away from outage by negligence. But sometimes Rory forgets.

'You got the wrong number – this is Mother Teresa.'

'It's still Mother Teresa,' I answer when the phone rings again.

'Hello, I –' But it's not Rory this time, it's Tsunami. 'This *is* you, isn't it?'

'It might be. Then again it might not.'

'I –' There's a pause; there's always a pause. 'You

haven't changed your mind, have you? About us, I mean?' When I don't reply, she continues. 'Look, I know not to use your name and I also know not to call you. But the other phones weren't responding so I ...'

The *Island Princess* is sliding through the Heads flanked by a couple of tugs. The big boat's got to go where the tugs take her and it's the same with Tsunami.

'Are you still there?' she asks.

'Yeah.'

'I'm afraid.'

'We're all afraid,' I say. 'It's called life. Where are you?'

'In the office.' Her voice descends to a whisper. 'Only I can't concentrate because of this fear. And it isn't *that* kind of fear. There's someone ... I'm not imagining it, someone really is –'

'Describe the *someone*.'

I hear shuffling on the other end of the Telefunken, like Tsunami's picking up pens and putting them down again, aimlessly.

'I – can't.'

Which means she only *thinks* that someone's tailing her.

'There's either someone or there isn't.'

'It's not as simple as that. As a soldier I learnt to ignore this sort of thing at my peril. People die for less. There's someone out there.'

Chapter 6

SPEAK HARD, SPEAKEASY

'There's someone out *where?*'

'Around the next corner or behind the last one, how should I know?'

'Is there something you haven't told me?'

'Only that I have to be on my guard.'

I know the feeling.

'So what is it?'

'I don't know. But I thought you'd care enough to check it out, to make sure I'm safe, I –'

'I'm a long way from where you are. By the time I got there, whoever it is will have gone.'

'Isn't there anyone you could send in your place?'

'No.'

The moment she hangs up, the phone does its *rat-a-tat-tat* again. It's Rory coming out of the queue.

'Why didn't you pick up?'

'What do you want?'

'I want to apologise for my behaviour that time. I was short.'

There's two counts and Roarer's right on both of them – he's five foot nothing and in the Cock Robin caper he wouldn't let me in out of the rain.

'Is that all?'

'No, I got a call.'

'And?'

'I can't say over the phone.'

I've bagged the empty whisky bottle and found myself a half-full one, the sunlight's sparkling on the Harbour, the job the Bertie kid dealt me can wait and before this it was shaping into a beautiful day. I sigh – like I told Tsunami, life doesn't come complete with a tape measure.

'Okay, we'll meet at the usual place. But before that, there's something I want you to do, seeing as you're feeling contrite.'

'Anything you want, mate,' he says. 'Just say the word.'

So – using code – I say the word.

The speakeasy's having one of its speak-hard days – there are a lot of cops while honest-to-goodness, bona fide, card-carrying criminals are thin on the ground. I enter under a sign saying *EAR* instead of *O'LEARY'S* because this is the Cross to find Hank the barman behind the counter but no sign of Rory.

Hank hands me a glass of green stuff with a little pink umbrella sticking out of it.

'If you listen hard enough you'll hear that drink talk. It's saying how nice it is you teamed the electric-blue jacket with the polka-dot tie, the orange hat and the snarl.'

I play along; there's nothing else to play. 'Why

does it say that?'

'Because it's complimentary.' I don't laugh and Hank keeps talking to cover his contusion. 'I expect you're looking for Rory.'

'He said he'd be here.' I nod in the direction of the clientele without looking; it pays to keep your head down even in O'Leary's; make that *especially* at O'Leary's. 'What's with all the fuzz?'

'Ever since that latest jihad incident, politicians of all persuasions have joined the fight against terrorism. People are afraid and politicians are anxious to translate that fear into votes. This' – he waves his cloth at the room – 'is the cutting edge of the fight against terrorism.'

I told Rory to do a job after which I'd meet him at O'Leary's but somewhere along the line he got side-tracked. I climb down off the stool.

'If Roarer shows,' I say, 'tell him I couldn't wait.'

In the Cock Robin caper, Tsunami was there when I needed her so I owe her one. I unstable the Heckler & Coalesce as I mount the stairs to the third floor of the refurbished brothel where she keeps her office to find a door with a black-and-white sign on it saying:

SUE MAHONEY
ENGINEERING – CIVIL
BUT ONLY IF YOU KNOCK BEFORE ENTERING

I don't do like the sign says. Do like the sign says and I could get knocked *after* entering – given the panic in Tsunami's voice when she telephoned; the fact that Rory didn't keep our rendezvous; and too much silence behind the sign to be good for anyone. I kick open the door, swivel and hit the floor on the dive.

If I say I didn't know what to expect I'd be lying. I knew what to expect only it's not what I get. Instead, there's a suite of offices got up like an army barracks – white as far as the eye can see, nothing on the white-painted walls and not much more in the way of furniture. No Rory, no Tsunami and not even the breath of a whisper they've been here. Just a desk with an electronic recorder on it which I pick up and switch on.

There's stuff about engineering, Tsunami dictating letters and writing reports – interspersed with Tsunami talking to herself. A lot of technical jargon before – out of the blue or the purple or the indigo or however you want to play it – the following: *Adults are no more than children writ tall.* The voice is indistinct; I can only just make out what she's saying. *What we become is engraved in our psyches right from the start. Don't talk to me about trauma – I've had enough to last a lifetime.* Silence, then: *This isn't what I signed up for. I thought I could have something with Rainbow but it's like he's running away, just like I am.*

It makes a lot of sense and it doesn't make any sense at all. There's a noise at the door and I swing round only to find it's static coming out of the recorder along with a voice saying the one word: *Rude.* It's Roarer with his phone-voice on, talking into his phone. *Rude,* he says. Then Tsunami to no-one in particular: *We have to go.* Followed by silence.

It takes me a while to work out the buttons. These things ain't like they used to be – a spool behind a window wearing a tape that you wind this way and that. Instead there's a lot of electronic buttonry. More snatches of Tsunami agonising about existence, more engineering specifications then, just when I'm about to give up, Roarer saying that one word again: *Rude.*

Only it's not *Rude* but *Rube.*

Chapter 7

HIS AND HEARSE

When I get to Rube's, I find a hearse at the kerb, the front door smashed in and the hall wearing eau-de-cologne. The torn-out pages of books – Dupont's *Blasters' Handbook* circa 1934, *The History of the Decline and Fall of the Roman Empire*, a *King James Bible*, R.B. Samuelson's *Detection Methods* and Roger Rogerson's *The Compleat Cabinetmaker* – litter the lounge. The safe's wide open and empty. The coffee table Rube took so much trouble to make is intact but the carpet's up and several floorboards have been prised away.

This was where Rube reared me on old Jimmy Cagney movies, ballet and detection methods after taking me out of school when the bullying got too much. It's also where she died. I know this from the silence, from the busted banisters and because – after her kidney transplant – Rube never went upstairs again. But she's upstairs now.

'Roarer?'

Silence.

'Roarer!'

More silence.

Then, 'I'm up here, mate.'

I take the stairs three at a time. The joint never looked lived-in but right now it looks died-in. Through the bathroom doorway I make out a dragged-down shower curtain and traces of blood. I straighten the black-framed photo of a group of kids in the hall. Rube's bedroom's at the end.

Her body's still warm. At the time of death, she was wearing a black T-shirt and jeans. I'm aware of Tsunami behind me as I turn to Rory.

'How did you know about it?'

Rory's as shaken as a bad martini.

'She rang just as I got to the dame's. Apparently she tried calling you but you were busy so she –'

'What did she say?'

'Something like –'

'The exact words, Roarer.'

Tsunami's looking from me to Rory and back again, anywhere but at the figure on the floor. She's seen death before but not like this – all her deaths wore uniforms.

'She said –' Rory frowns; he's used to killing strangers, not downloading obituaries on people close to him. 'She said, *Is that you, Rory?*'

'Jesus, Roarer …'

'You asked for her exact words and that's what she said.'

I resist killing him; one death's enough.

'Go on.'

'I said *Is that you, Rube?* And she repeated: *Is that you, Rory?* And I said: *Yeah.* Then there was a lot of noise after which she said –'

'Describe the noise.'

'A door getting smashed in and a couple of shots.'
'What kind of shots?'
'.25 slugs out of a Baby Browning.'
Rube toted a Baby Browning because – along with the matches for the stove and her handkerchief – at just over four inches, the peashooter fitted neatly into the pocket of her apron. Under the circumstances it would have been as useful as a popgun against Godzilla.
'What did she say after you confirmed your identity?'
'I could only make out one word – it started with *N*.'
'That's it? An entire conversation and that's all you remember?'
The colour drains from Rory's face. 'It wasn't a word I was familiar with. It sounded – foreign. Besides which I had to move fast and the dame insisted on accompanying me.'
I check my watch.
'Rube's been dead over an hour. The cops respond slow but eventually they'll turn up and we don't want to be around when they do.'
Downstairs I straighten the hall table, write Imogene's name, address and phone number on the back of her photo and remove the camera. It comes out easy – the *obscura* one in the middle of the wall, not the obvious one sitting up and saying *Take me*, which is what the intruders did. The coffee table comes apart the way Rube designed it to. I slide out the pegs holding the outer cover in place and discard the top until what I'm left with is a filing cabinet – a lightweight box made of three-ply timber about the

size and shape of a baby's coffin.

We're pulling away from the kerb when the TV crew arrives. A TV crew?

'Couldn't you have chosen something a bit more obvious than a hearse, Roarer? Why not a screaming-pink van with a loudspeaker sticking out of the top announcing: *We're speeding away from a murder, come and get us?*'

Rory's got the lights on – or maybe the lights come on automatic in hearses – and traffic's lining up obediently behind us. I tell Tsunami to get on the floor, after which I pull my fedora over my eyes and slide down in my seat. Rory shrugs or maybe he's just having trouble with the pedals.

'How was I to know there'd be a murder? This hearse is my daily drive and the fact that I'm driving it is – what's the word – no more than continental.'

'Coincidental.'

The answer's automatic because my mind's elsewhere. What's with the TV people? They must have been just around the corner sipping lattés. I try to block Rube's body out of my mind. *You can't solve cases through a vale of tears,* she'd say. Or maybe it was *veil. You have to stay objective – check my wounds; close my mouth; cover me if I'm uncovered; destroy the hard drive; write the kid's name and address on the back of her photograph; and take the little wooden filing cabinet built into the coffee table in the middle of the room where everyone can see it and take it for granted – take it for granted and therefore not take it* ...

Roarer's still banging on about the hearse. 'It's bulletproof, there's two rows of seats and it holds two coffins – it's even got a place for your tinnies.'

'But why a hearse?'

'When I gave up killing, the Singalong Church gave me obsolescence for my sins in return for my life's savings, leaving me with nothing to survive on but my wits.' I don't say anything. 'A man's got to make a living.'

'How can you make a living driving a *hearse*?'

We're taking the back roads. There are still cameras but they're not so prevalent.

Roarer shrugs. 'I buy and sell old American cars: Dodges, de Sotos, Buicks, Chevrolets, Caddies ...'

'Is it legit?'

'It doesn't pay that good so it must be.'

Chapter 8

PLAY IT AGAIN

Rory's place is where it's always been – on the wrong side of the tracks in the wrong suburb at the wrong end of a wrong city. The driveway contains a black Buick Electra, a pink Chevrolet Biscayne, a grey Olds and a purple-and-green Lincoln Continental. The furniture's covered with cobwebs and black mould's giving a come-as-you-are party on the southern elevation. I set Rube's box on the lounge-room floor.

'Where's Janet?' I ask.

Roarer shrugs. 'She found religion.'

'I thought she'd already found religion.'

'All right, she ran off with the minister.'

That's why he wants to be friends again.

'You mean that fat bugger who hitched you?'

Roarer looks uncomfortable. Roarer always looks uncomfortable but right now he looks like he's playing host to a plague of fleas.

'When I caught them at it he said it was no more than a *laying-on of hands.*'

I leave it at that; there's nowhere else to leave it.

'You got a machine I can watch a video on?'

Rory leads me to a hole under the house.

'This was our little joke,' he explains. 'Janet didn't like me under her feet.' The entrance is via a crawl-hatch from the side path and there's an air vent I can see the street through. 'So I ended up under her feet – how erotic's *that*?'

'You mean *ironic*.'

'That's what I said.'

I change the subject. 'What happens to the house?'

'The Church is selling it off which means I got to excavate.'

'When?'

'They're taking the furniture today.'

Tsunami appears in the hatchway, beautiful in black.

'I got to get back to work. Can someone call me a cab?'

'You're a cab,' Rory says. When no-one laughs he shrugs. 'I'll take you in the hearse.'

Rube's box contains details of all her cases, recorded in handwriting as precise as her mind. From the very first words of the first entry – *MISSING PERSONS* – it's like she comes to life again: *A runaway's like a soldier absent without leave: a look of bewilderment on the parents' faces, suspicion in that of the lover, confusion among friends and – nine times out of ten – a couldn't-care-less attitude on the part of the police. There's no body, no crime scene, no murder weapon, no suspect and it's a big country. It's as if the person never*

existed ...

I flick through to the file labelled *ERRANT SPOUSES*. First page: *The politicians promised that infidelity would end with no-fault divorce but it simply means people like me no longer burst into cheap hotel rooms telling people to smile for the dicky-bird. Straying husbands and wives are as prevalent as ever ...*

I'm kneeling among the ruins of Rory's marriage surrounded by my Aunt's files when a shock runs through me. *Pay attention to those feelings,* Rube said. *They're the warnings that an animal gets before an earthquake, subliminal sensations we so-called civilised beings ignore because we think we're above them.* The file marked *PERSONAL* starts like one of those signs on the backs of cars that read: *If you can read this you're too damn close.*

If you're reading this it's because I no longer exist ... The words conjure up hard-to-handle memories because – just like the sign says – I'm too close. A note falls out. *This little filing cabinet – overlooked because it was right under my killers' noses – contains details of all my cases. Among the notes you'll discover who killed me. I don't know who it was – if I had known, I could have prevented my death. I'd rather you moved on, Rainbow, but knowing you, you won't. Apart from which, if my prognosis is right, they'll be after you, too. Which means you'll have to do what's necessary to protect you and yours. But first watch the video.*

In the hole in the wall under Roarer's joint I insert the cassette and hit *PLAY.* Enter, *Left,* Rube, wearing an apron. She moves out of shot towards kitchen, returns, paces up and down like she's forgotten the cameras or – like any good actor – is simply pretending they don't exist. Beyond her, the door's still where it's meant to be.

Suddenly she frowns. I stop the video, wind back – watching her jerk about like she's being volted – and start the tape on its forward progress again. As she frowns, Rube glances down. I pause the video on the downward flick of her eyes, note the time in the bottom right-hand corner, then hit *Unpause*. Rube bends, picks up the receiver from the telephone in the hall, speaks into it, listens, speaks some more, listens some more, then finally hangs up. *Note facial expression.* Hit *Play*. She seems to consider something then come to a decision. She feels in her apron for the gun.

I force myself to keep watching. Rube disappears. To reappear five minutes later clad in jeans and T-shirt and carrying a basket. An hour later – I've fast-forwarded – she returns through the front door with her basket full of goodies. I can only see what's on top of the basket: a half-pound of Sourco butter; d'Aura coffee; a newspaper – Rube loved her newspapers – folded to show part of a headline that starts *TERRORIST THREAT TO* ... while a baguette's dangling over the side of the basket like it wants to escape.

She disappears in the direction of the kitchen and I fast-forward the tape before bringing the speed back to *Normal*. I'm not looking for clues because the killers haven't arrived yet. Watching the video is a means of keeping Rube alive, like calling my daughter to tell her I've got a new phone number, on the off-chance my ex-wife will let me speak to her. But I'll never hear Rube's voice again.

The cloth on the hall table rises like a ghost's lifting it – the barest of flutters. But it's the breeze before the tornado, the flutter of butterfly wings that ends in a storm, a presage of doom. Suddenly, the front door's on the floor and figures are swarming across it. Rube goes for her mosquito-blaster but she's too late – she's slowed since the kidney transplant – and the lead figure catches her by the arm so that her pea shots go wide, smacking harmlessly into the jamb and the wall beside it while leaving the intruders intact.

I wind back and play it again – only this time on *Slow*. Again the cloth flutters, again the door bulges and again Rube goes for her gun. I shift attention from Rube to the intruders. To find they're wearing anonymous clothes while their faces are pixilated – hair covered, noses squashed, ears crushed and eyes and mouths the vaguest of shapes – by the cut-off feet of panty-hose.

My mind's between the morgue and a hard place when I hear the sound of a motor being cut, doors slamming, feet on the front steps, a key turning in the lock and footsteps on the floor above. I stop the video and peer through the peep-hole. From the lounge room comes the slip-slide of furniture being moved, the footsteps heavier now because they're weighted by their load, then the soft thud of a couch hitting a wall. *The Church is selling the house so I got to excavate. When? They're taking the furniture today.* The Telefunken rings and I click on before the removalists can hear it. The voice at the other end is querulous.

'Daddy?'

Once I had more than one kid. Before I discovered that two were fathered by a telephone repairman while the fourth was a concoction of my imagination – a vain attempt to resuscitate my dead sister.

'Yes, darling?'

I call her *darling* because – after all these years – I can still get the name wrong. Just the name – not the kid. Because I know who it is, can see her broad as daylight, my little girl – make that grown woman because Imogene must be all of eighteen now, or maybe twenty – clutching the phone and sobbing, 'Daddy, Auntie Rube's dead!'

Chapter 9

BETWEEN THE MORGUE
AND A HARD PLACE

I don't tell her I already know and that *she* only knows because I wrote her name, address and telephone number on the back of a photo on the hall table I left for the cops.

'Are you still there, Daddy? They said someone killed Auntie Ruby and Mummy was awful about it – shouting at the police because she thought they were only here because of you. Daddy?'

'I'm still here, sweetheart.'

'Why are you whispering?'

'The news must have affected my vocal cords. Go on.'

'They took her to the – you-know-where – and as next of kin they want me to identify the body. Can we meet somewhere?'

'I can't go to the morgue because of the cops.'

'What about afterwards?'

'Where afterwards?'

She tells me where afterwards, in code.

God moves in mysterious ways but there's no guarantee He'll do it quiet. Upstairs, the crashing and banging says the removalists are getting on with their removalling and through the vent in the wall I can see a pantechnicon with the words *SAVOES DEPOT* on it, the back door's open and a man wearing a tag that says *TED* is loading a chair.

She's wearing faded blue jeans and a fashionably ragged top and with her hair cropped short I barely recognise her. Standing on the other side of Parramatta Road, her eyes fixed on the hedge, she doesn't look like her mother – which is a blessing. But neither does she look like me – which is even more of a blessing. She's got one foot forward and her arms out like I taught her and her face is pale because she's just come from seeing Aunt Rube.

The morgue's at the back of the Coroner's Court in a suburb with no trees called Forest Lodge. Through the hedge, I see cops barging through the automagic doors. Inside, they park their bo-diddlies in the lockers provided and – after giving evidence to the Coroner – retrieve their gats, return to their cars and drive away. Other players include lawyers, witnesses, clerks, secretaries, suspects, hangers-on and – on a big day – TV crews. This must be a big day.

Imogene crosses the street just like any other kid except instead of having wires sticking out of her ears she's busy noting age, sex and danger level of fellow pedestrians – ever-ready to reach into her open-necked casement bag for the pepper pot.

That's when she sees me and that's when her eyes light up and she forgets all her training and starts running.

And for a moment I forget everything I ever learnt, too, and suddenly she's in my arms and laughing. 'Daddy!' she cries. 'My little girl,' I say back ...

Only that's in my imagination. Because in reality she looks right, left and dead centre, after which she walks slowly across the road and – while still a pace away – stops and we shake hands like strangers.

Pandora could be behind the tree by the oval or secreted next to the hedge. Rube's dead and even if Pandora didn't do it, it's like the blade's already between my scapulae and I don't know how I'm still on my feet. Imogene stares like I'm a mirage and I take one of those breaths that mirages take.

'We should spend more time together, kid.' That's as intimate as it gets. 'Did you do the ID?'

She nods. 'It was Auntie Rube all right. She always said it could happen.' Again the stare. 'You knew before I called you, didn't you?'

'I couldn't identify her without revealing my own identity, Immo – a faceless man can't do IDs.' I change the subject. 'What's with all the cameras?'

'Something to do with terrorists. They wanted to interview me but I gave them the slip.'

'How's school?'

Once more, the stare. 'You know I've left school, Daddy.' Imogene hurries over the implications of my not knowing. 'I'm eighteen now, which means I can make my own decisions.'

Yesterday she was a babe in arms, today she's making decisions.

'So what are you up to?'

'I'm ... at uni.'

From the moment they're born you wonder what

will happen to them. Imogene was never going to be nothing. I can't keep the complacency out of my voice when I ask, 'And what are you studying – at uni?'

'You'll be upset.'

'I don't get upset.'

'It's not university in the *traditional* sense.' She can't meet my gaze. 'I've enrolled in the – I'm attending the Police Academy in Goulburn.'

The traffic on Parramatta Road ceases to exist and I struggle to breathe. It wasn't my worst fear because it was never a possibility.

'You mean you got to study for *that*?' I'm on the side of the angels but nine times out of ten the angels aren't; my job's to fill in the gaps left by the cops and sometimes the gaps are chasms; I step back; it's not a conscious act but that only makes it worse. 'For God's sake, Immo – *why*?'

She's got a lot of reasons – too many. Foremost among them is Rube's death; Imogene had already pretty much decided when it happened but Rube's death made it a certainty. Somewhere amid all the explanations is the need to do good and while she's talking I find myself thinking: *I should have stayed with the mother, toughed out the marriage, been there to protect the kid.* Except that maybe it was me Imogene needed protecting from. She's still explaining when I cut across her.

'You got nothing to apologise for, Immo. But I suppose if they knew you had someone like me for a father …'

'You are what you are, Daddy.'

What did I expect – harps and fairies? I hunch my

shoulders and make the best of a bad job.

Chapter 10

THE CASE MAN

'Let me give you a piece of advice, Immo. When you're –' the words stick in my throat '– when you're what you're going to be, you got to stay on the side of the angels, do you hear me? You don't have to do me any favours – never mind I'm your Dad. Lesson number one in law enforcement is to avoid bias – no helping family, knock-ons for friends or kickbacks to chance acquaintances. Crookedness starts with good intentions and ends in evil. There's no such thing as *half*-bent.' I think about that. 'At least you're not turning criminal, Immo.'

She smiles a wan smile and her eyes are glistening but it's still a smile. 'I forgot to tell you – that's next.' The smile fades. 'Don't worry, I'm still me. And when you finally come to terms with what I'm doing, you'll realise you're partly responsible.' I imagine her in uniform, complete with gun, hit-stick, stunner, handcuffs and the walk – especially the walk. 'What do you want to do now?'

I'd like to stay friends, that's what I want to do now. Which means that I got to work out how I won't be an embarrassment to her – but only after I find out who killed Rube.

'Like they say in the song, Immo: *You go your way and I'll go mine; now and forever till the end of time.* I'll just finish this case I'm working on, after which I'll …'

Imogene interrupts. 'I never told you this, Daddy, but that was my name for you – *The Case Man*. It's what I called a doll I had. The doll had a tough face and I dressed him in the sort of clothes you wear – you know, kind of crappy – and went to him for advice. I asked him about becoming a cop.'

'And what was his reply?'

'He said what you want to say, Daddy, but can't – *Go for it, kid.* So that's what I'm doing. What's the case?'

'I need to find out who killed Rube.'

I don't tell her about the other case, the one I'm doing for the Thomas kid.

'But that's police work!'

I shake my head; the body in the morgue used to be Rube. 'To the cops, Rube's death is nothing more than a difficult case closed. They never liked her because she exposed their shortcomings. So all they'll do is punch their fists in the air and shout *That's one for the goodies!* I got to do it, Immo.'

'But isn't that what you've always told me to do, keep the *personal* out of what should be objective – don't do things for family, et cetera?' She hasn't even started and she's already struggling. 'Can't you give up detecting? I want you to live. I've just lost Rube – I don't want to lose you, too.'

My mind's on the clock and I know the kid knows because even as we're talking she's moving further away – both physically and emotionally. Growing up's another way of saying *growing away*. And all the time Pandora's behind, beside or in front of me, awaiting her moment because she knows it's getting close.

'Just this one last case, Sweetheart.'

But Imogene's already turned her back and – slinging her bag casually over her shoulder but always ready to reach into it for the spray – is walking out of my life and into her own.

Like I told Harry, everything's connected. Which includes the headlines screaming: *TERRORISTS STRIKE AGAIN*, *Well-known Female Investigator Struck Down in Blind Jihad* and *HOW LONG MUST WE COP THIS LOT?* When I get back to Rube's, the blue-and-white tape's in place and the door's nailed shut but there's something cursory about it, like they've just gone through the paces, because it's only the death of an old woman.

In the photograph she's leaning against a lamppost with her arms crossed, frowning into the sun. 'She walked like it hurt and she was wearing a T-shirt and jeans and carrying a basket.'

The café proprietor's got better things to do with his time than look at pictures of old women.

'When was I supposed to have seen her?'

I shrug. 'When you saw her.'

Black shirt, blacker look and he couldn't give a damn about anything except making coffee and money.

'If it was lunchtime I was busy.'

'She was murdered.'

'I was still busy.'

I indicate the waitress behind him. 'She might have seen something.'

'She's working.'

'That makes two of us.'

The overblown barista taps his watch to show who's in charge and his frown warns the waitress: *Take more than five minutes over this and you're out on your sweet potato.*

'What's your name?'

'Jane.'

'Have you seen this woman before, Jane?'

'Of course I have. That's dear old Rube. Why, what happened to her?'

'Why should anything happen to her?'

'Because you're showing me her photograph and you've got that look on your face. Besides, I *knew* something might happen because I saw this man and had a flash of implication.'

'You mean *insight*.'

'Whatever it was I had a flash of it. He seemed interested in Rube.'

'Describe him.'

'He was leaning against the wall of the old jail. I knew he wasn't a local because his shoes were clean.'

'What did he look like, under the clothes?'

'A cross between a lawyer and an assassin. You still haven't told me what happened.'

'She was murdered.'

Hand to mouth, eyes wide with horror – passes reaction test.

Final question. 'Do you recall the expression on her face?'

'She looked worried. I only say that because –'

'– usually she never looked worried?'

Bone, the dame in the flower shop on the corner, The Greenhouse Defect, remembers Rube hurrying past with her head down while a dero saw a late-model black BMW outside the laundromat. The woman in the deli thought Rube seemed preoccupied – she had to remind her to buy butter. And the phone records indicate that, just before she went shopping – I don't know the details, my contact could only provide the metadata – Rube had a 1 minute 21 second conversation with a stranger.

Chapter 11

THE HUNTSMAN

The past's a huntsman. Huntsmen are spiders that finagle their way into penny-slot gaps to become part of the furniture. Until one day you open the door and they fall on your face when you least expect it.

'Imogene's gone,' Salina says through her tears.

'Yeah, she said.'

'Police officers get killed in the line of duty which means she's going to die.' I'm standing well back so she can't hit me. 'And *you're* to blame.'

'Come on, Sal, you know I hate the fuzz.'

'That's why she signed up, out of rebellion against you.'

I'm not going to argue. Arguing with my ex is like wrestling with glue. We're up a side alley with too many spiders in it.

'Look, Sal, I'm not here to talk about Imogene; I'm interested in Clint.'

Clint was the telephone repairman who came to plug in our phone and ended up plugging Salina. At the same time, he was also making connections with several other women – a fact that Sal discovered after obtaining his phone records from another Telco employee.

'Clint's dead,' she says bluntly.

The fact that Clint had been boffing Salina while she was my wife gave me a hold over him – enough to get the phone records that helped nail a killer. The only problem from Clint's point of view was that he was killed in the process.

'Rube got a phone call just before she died. I need to know the identity of the caller; your contact – the one who obtained Clint's phone records – could tell me who it was.'

My ex-wife considers me through her tears. 'And after I tell you, will you leave me alone?'

I tell her *Yes*.

'Her name's Marianne Merriman. She's got a social conscience.'

The dame across the table is smarter than she looks but that's because I'm the one doing the looking. She takes a swig of her expensive wine and when she glances around at the equally expensive diners, I can make out the indentation left by the headset.

'All these rich bastards.' Her peepers swivel back to me. 'Why do you want that telephone number?'

'It'll help solve the murder of a little old lady.'

'What you're asking me to do is illegal.'

'Most of life's illegal, Merriman.' She's bright, bored and possessed of a social conscience; I gamble on the character assessment. 'Do you play chess?'

'What's chess got to do with the price of a good feed?'

'Chess is about good versus evil. Sometimes black wins and sometimes white loses but in the end it always comes down to good versus evil.'

'It's only a game.'

'Not when you're playing. When you're playing, the pieces are real, their removal from the board is real and – win or lose – the game's for keeps.'

She looks up from her chicken.

'You talk about pieces – bishops, rooks and the rest. What about the pawns?'

I've told the waiters to keep the food coming and it's the kind of joint where they do what you tell them as long as you pay. I hunch over my salad.

'Look at these big spenders and remember that – unlike them – me and you and people like us are no more than those self-same pawns, only able to move one square at a time. Unless, of course, you're smart enough to take a piece *en passant* – that is, move more than one square and take out a big one. That's what I'm offering you – a chance to strike a blow for the little man – sorry, *person*. A call was made, someone died and that someone was my aunt – a white pawn who took on the army of the night and lost.'

Merriman can tuck it away. But she can also listen because it's her job to listen. 'How do you know I'm not one of the bad people?' she says.

I shrug. 'Good and bad are in the eye of the beholder. That's why there's so much trouble in the world – everyone thinks they're right. And the more right they think they are, the more dangerous they become.'

Marianne Merriman smiles, nods, mops up the rest of her gravy, cleans up her ice-cream and palms me the number.

You got two choices when you get a number like this – you can either chuck it in the nearest bin and forget about it, or you can die. I call the number.

Immediately a voice says, 'You're ringing from an untraceable phone. I can respond only after you advise me of your identity.'

'You'll respond if I tell you my call concerns terrorism.'

'How do I know what you're telling me is true?'

'Because of today's headlines. I'm on the side of peace and I need details of a conversation.'

I give the name of the *callee* – Rube – plus the date, time and duration of the conversation.

'Sorry, but we're bound by law to collect no more than the dates and times of calls and who called whom. Which appears to be information that you already have.'

'Tell that to the birds. As it happens, I'm not the birds.'

The voice doesn't miss a beat. 'Where do you want to meet?'

If you're playing a Grand Master, you need to think several moves ahead just to stay in the game. I do the equivalent of crossing a river in flood in order to shake off a pack of tracker dogs.

'The Martin Place memorial in half an hour. Bring what I want and come alone.'

'How did you get my number?'

I click off.

The ordinary-looking joker in a grey T-shirt and even greyer jeans is in place. So, too, are the three snipers – one on the roof of the Uncommon Wealth Bank, one in the Post Office clocktower and the third mingling with the populace. The Grey Man's head shoots up when I ring him.

'You're calling from another untraceable phone.'

I ignore the protest. 'I told you to come alone.'

He thinks quick but that's how he's paid to think.

'I didn't invite him – the back-up's the Agency's *default* option.'

'Nice try but I count at least three of them.'

'Yeah, well, like I say, I –'

'Next stop Centennial Park.'

'But that's several hundred acres of parkland!'

'Wait by one of the gates. I'll find you. You'll get further instructions on arrival. And this time, no shooters.'

Chapter 12

MURDER BOYS

Roarer's driving a stolen Fiat.

'Does this mean we're mates again, Rain?'

'No, it means I need someone with a stolen Fiat.'

The Grey Man's opted for the Lang Road gates because they provide plenty of hidey-holes. There's no sign of back-up but that just means the gunmen are better hidden than they were last time. I watch as he clicks on and read his lips as he mouths the word *Ready!* into his wristwatch.

'I want you standing by the kerb, Grey Man,' I say into the phone; he takes a step, all the time looking about him. 'Closer – so close you might be stormwater on your way to the Harbour.'

We come at him from the eastern end, Roarer slowing just enough for me to scoop up the Grey Man and hibernate him. After which Rory accelerates as the wolverines come down from the fold.

I've relieved the Grey Man of everything right down to his recorder pen; his tracker bracelet's at the bottom of the Harbour; and we've ditched the Fiat. I didn't need to remove his powers of conversation because he never had any.

'I chucked all your belongings in the Harbour.'

'Then you've just signed your death warrant,' he says. 'Australia's counter-terrorism powers are second to none. We'll work out who you are and track you down, even though you're hiding your identity behind a hijab.'

I consider him through my peep-hole. 'It's a burqa not a hijab. And you can't trace me because I'm an unknown quantity. And when you fail to find me you'll look even worse than you do now.' I shrug. 'But I'm prepared to give you an alibi if you drop the *mucho-macho* and give me what I want.'

'Which is?'

'What I asked for – the transcript of a conversation.'

'It's in the sole of one of the sneakers that you chucked in the Harbour.'

I produce the sneaker; it's empty.

'Nice try but I didn't and it wasn't. Your latest lie leaves me no choice but to make you look even more stupid than you do already. You, the great protector of people's freedom, have been abducted. Do you want to be tarred and feathered as well and left in the middle of Bondi? It'd be the end of a promising career.'

'I committed the transcript to memory.'

I produce his recorder pen and click on.

'So now you can uncommit it.'

After we dump the spook, Rory says he wants another job so I tell him to keep an eye on Harry. Then I get back to the boat where I pour a Glenfiddich, take out the spook's recorder pen and hit *Play*. The voice is *tremolo* but otherwise the words flow nice because the Grey Man's got no cause to lie. While he's talking I conjure up the image of Rube looking worried.

*TRANSCRIPT OF CONVERSATION BETWEEN AGENCY AND OCCASIONAL AGENT R***:*

MALE VOICE: I have an urgent message for you.

*R***: Who's this?*

VOICE: You know who it is.

*R***: Why are you breaking cover?*

VOICE: You've helped us in the past so now we're helping you.

*R***: What's the message?*

VOICE: They're coming to get you and we cannot — repeat cannot — come to your aid. Which means that you're on your own. Leave immediately and do not return in the foreseeable future. Go shopping or fly to the moon but leave and do not return. I repeat: we're powerless to help you.

I play it again till I've got it by heart. After which I drop the recorder over the side for the fishes to listen to. Important phrases: *we cannot come to your aid; you're on your own; we're powerless to help you*. It's not necessary to analyse the voice — I know who it is.

I watch the Harbour go about its innocent business – ferries, yachts, seagulls – under the so-called protection of our counter-terrorism agencies. Since when were such people *powerless*? More to the point: what could make them that way?

I put on the flak jacket under the coat and because someone's tailing me take the long way to Rory's. When I arrive, I make two phone calls; the second one's to Rory. I keep to code and Roarer responds in kind.

'Does this mean we're mates again?'

'No.'

When he arrives he's behind the wheel of the hearse and he's sweating a dog's smile; I shove aside his crutch and climb in.

'What's the news on Harry?' I ask.

'He's going about his business.'

'No sign of trouble?'

'Not that I could see.'

'Keep watching.'

But Roarer's mind has moved on; it's not much of a mind but it moves. The last time I needed help he slammed the door in my face.

'Look, if you're still cranky about that door business, Rain, let me just say I didn't have any choice.' We're heading south by south-west. 'I was trying to make my marriage work and you were a good part of the reason it didn't. You got to learn to turn the other lip, Rain, because God moves in mysterious ways, his blunders to perform.'

'It's *wonders* not *blunders*, Roarer – which is another way of saying that people don't need to worry because Someone Else is picking up the pieces.' I shake my head. 'God or Allah or Jehovah or whatever He calls Himself twigged early on to the fact that knowledge is power – which is why He operates on a *need-to-know* basis.'

Rory changes gears, his one foot flying, his face frowning. 'I did all that church stuff but I still don't get it. Maybe it's because I've got gunfire-induced industrial deafness. I only realised afterwards that the fat bugger in the bullpit –'

'Pulpit.'

'– was saying *God willing*, not *God killing*, and that the song didn't go *Murder boys* but *Gird her loins*.' He taps the wheel. 'I guess people hear what they want to hear.'

'Right.'

'I know I'm bloody right, Rain. When that fat bugger started adulterating Janet …'

'I said *right* as in *turn right*!'

Rory flicks the wheel and veers in front of a truck that clips the sign on the back of the hearse reading *FUNERAL IN PROGRESS*. The funeral was nearly ours.

Chapter 13

THE CEMENT MEN

The sign above the gate reads *HEA-VAN ON EARTH* but grass won't grow where grass won't grow and at some stage they called in the cement men. The joker behind the counter pretends to check the books – they always pretend to check the books – and when he looks up he's in lockdown.

'No vacancies,' he says.

I'm wearing the bright blue coat with the gold fleck in it, the tough expression and the hat. If I was him I wouldn't have any vacancies either.

'I'll pay double.'

Suddenly he's got a vacancy.

Going by the prices, the cement's rolled gold but the caravan's a roof over my head and he didn't demand any proof of identity.

KEEP QUITE and *ELECTRICS EXTRA*, the signs say. Along with *WATER TO BE PAYED FOR* and *CLEAN BOG AFTER USE*. I open Rube's file on the little flop-down table under the light I'm paying extra for to find three clipped-together sheets of A4 paper in a sealed, clear-plastic sleeve marked *WILL* and *WON'T.* The testament's short and there are no surprises. You can't make bequests to people that don't exist so Rube left everything to Imogene.

I hear movement but in caravan parks there's always movement – people arriving and people *de*riving; relationships breaking up and relationships breaking in; drunks drinking; lovers loving; residents showering or using the lavatory; dogs, cats, possums and mothers-in-law doing what dogs, cats, possums and mothers-in-law do. Except that whoever's outside is no mother-in-law – he's too furtive. Rube's dead and her killers were never going to leave it at that.

The other thing about caravans is they haven't got escape hatches. There's a little round sink; a table and seat that convert into a bed; a stove; a refrigerator; and a cupboard. And someone outside.

I check the cupboard but all it contains is an iron, an ironing board, a lot of mould and the usual ragged pile of *Phantom* comics. To satisfy the law, vans have got wheels. Which means they tend to bounce in response to movement so I stay where I am. Whoever's out there saw me come in so they know what I'm wearing. A change of clothes will give me a lifesaving moment of uncertainty.

I take off my hat and coat but keep the flak jacket. *Coming ready or not.* Because if I stay where I am, bullets will find me. All the gunman has to do is rake back and forth until he hears the screams that say he hit me. After which he'll hit me some more.

I think it through like Rube must have thought it through, but without the flak jacket. When I open the door he'll have a target and it'll be my chest and that's what he'll aim for – the biggest and brightest of all available targets: me in the brightly lit doorway, all dressed up like a shish-kebab. And if he's a good enough shot there's a chance I'll live because he'll hit the flak jacket. I shovel the *WILL* and *WON'T* back in the box before hauling out the Heckler & Cock.

Instead of taking the paces I do a jeté. I hear rustling as I throw open the door that tells me I've got surprise on my side. The volley – it comes late but it still comes – finds its mark. The gun's an AKS-74U – I know that because the bullets are 5.45 millimetre, not 9s. I hurl myself down and sideways out of the van, taking my weight on my left forearm while keeping my gun hand well out of trouble before turning the movement into a roll and ending up on my stomach in the prone-fire position.

Only there's nothing to prone-fire at. *When you're caught by surprise, don't move* – that's the code of the professional shooter and this shooter's nothing if not professional. The cement's making more movement than he is. Another rustle as a creature heads for some nocturnal rendezvous but otherwise –

I roll to the right – hard and fast – as a new batch of slugs seeks their target. We both know he outguns me; we also both know there's nothing to hide behind. The night scope means he can see everything except my thoughts.

CLEAN BOG AFTER USE. It's the only building of any substance – built of breeze blocks, low-flying but high enough to do the job if I can make it. But he knows where I am, the bullets will reach me before I'm halfway to safety and there'll be a levy on the surviving residents to pay for the clean-up. So I dive in the opposite direction. Feint and dive, then feint and dive some more as the salvos find their mark. Only it's the wrong mark, a bush halfway between where I was a split-second ago and the ablutions block.

The shooter forgot to kill the lights. Also too late, he realises that, while the power-saving bulbs are weak, they still shed enough illumination for me to see by. And also too late he finds out I'm armed.

He throws himself sideways. I could go for the kill but the sirens are closing in at fifty paces a second and when they arrive I don't want them to find a corpse – the shooter's or mine. So I clip his nearside capella and it's enough to make him scream but not so bad that he won't be able to escape. Which he's intent on doing because he knows he's missed his chance and will have to wait for the next one because he can hear the sirens, too.

Ten seconds – five. It doesn't matter about the bag but I've got to get Rube's box. I shelve the gat, get myself back inside the van, grab the little plywood coffin and I'm away just as the squaddies squeal through the gates.

The hearse is in shadow – a long, dark shape with Rory at the wheel.

'What are you doing here?'

He shrugs. 'Mates aren't something you put on and take off like your underpants, Rain. I thought you'd need help — call it a killer's *premeditation*.'

Tsunami's wearing men's pyjamas, she's been watching the television news and she doesn't seem all that surprised to see me.

'There's been a terrorist shootout in a caravan park,' she says. 'They're interviewing the manager now.'

'He was a terrorist, dead set, I knew it the moment I set eyes on him.'

The moron's saying what he'd want to hear if he was watching. *I only let him have the van because I knew he'd kill me if I didn't. When I heard the shots I immediately called the police.'*

He likes his world to look secure even if it isn't; his park's been shot up but that's not what he's on about.

'I was concerned for the residents — clearly they were in danger. Who knows with these people?'

The residents of the *HEA-VAN ON EARTH* caravan park were no longer slide-bys but so many law-abiding citizens.

'That's why I called in the cops.' The camera pans to the shot-up van. *'And what did the police do?'* the reporter asks. *'Were they able to make an arrest?'*

Tsunami switches off the TV. 'Nice to see you again,' she says. 'Where have you been?'

'In a caravan park.'

There was the Tsunami I first met – acting like she owned the world – who became a figure in black who might have been anyone. All I knew about her was that she was an ex-marine who understood trouble. Then she was on the boat cringing from too many ugly memories and after that, a lonely voice on a recorder. And now she's a dame in pyjamas.

She asks if I'll be comfortable before making herself scarce. This is Balmain where noise is cushioned by so much money that, however loud the noise, it still sounds like autumn leaves falling on lawn. No-one followed the hearse. Which should be a comfort, except that the one thing I'm sure of right now is that I can't be sure of anything. The world might stop but sooner or later the music will start again and the world will start turning again and – whether I like it or not – I'll have to move right along with it.

Rube's file still says: *RAINBOW – FOR YOUR EYES ONLY.* And after that: *If you're reading this it only means one thing and that is that I'm dead. I know I had it coming. But you'll have to find the people who did it because they'll be after you now. You'll have seen the CCTV but if these people run true to form, the cameras will tell you nothing.*

Later: *Some people see death as an end while for others it's only the beginning. But to me death's the start of what I like to call 'death duties' – the corpse's responsibility to those left behind.*

And still later: *Taking you on wasn't a burden, Rainbow, I don't want you ever to think that — it was a privilege. You offered the chance for me to change my life for the better. Maybe I only made things worse but I tried. It was no chore — I had fun, my little James Cagney, a great deal of fun …*

It's only words but they're almost too hard to bear.

NOTE: From time to time I do work for the Agency. I've been in touch with them regarding the present case. They say there are wheels within wheels as they always do in such cases and I'm not sure that the right hand knows what the left hand's doing. They owe me but there's nothing in writing. They did promise that when I was in mortal danger they'd warn me but what's that worth when you're in mortal danger?

Chapter 14

DEATH IN THE AFTERNOON

I stuff Rube's *PERSONAL* file in an inside pocket, pick up the box and when I open the door the peace of Balmain sweeps over me like sweet-scented balm. Tsunami's huddled next to me in a green woolly dressing gown. I explain why I'm leaving but she isn't listening.

'I thought you came here to – you know – make up for last time,' she says.

I clutch the box.

'I just needed a temporary haven, Tsunami. I'll get out of your hair.'

'When will you be back?'

For a moment, during which my going doesn't seem necessary, I decide to leave the detective business, settle down in a little house with Tsunami and have marzipan for tea. But that's before I remember I don't exist and that, if I try to settle down, Tsunami won't exist either. Because they'll find me – the ones I know, the ones I don't know and Pandora. Why am I thinking about sweet-scented balm? I've got a case to solve.

'I won't be back, Tsunami – at least, not in that

sense.'

'Then you can go to hell.'

I don't know how long they've been tailing me but after I cab it from Balmain to Likeheart, I find a bus stop with a bus in it by which means I hope to lose them. I want to put as much confusion between them and Tsunami as I can but the bus driver's decided I need help with the confusion.

'No coffins on government buses, pal,' he says, indicating the box.

'It's not a coffin.'

'You got a ticket?'

'I'll buy one.'

'You can't buy tickets on government buses any more – you need a prepaid card.' He gets a look on his face. 'That's two strikes against you – the coffin and the card. And if we had dress regulations you'd score the trifecta.'

Argue the toss with this joker and he'll call the cops. Which is how I find myself taking the back streets and that's when I see them again. They've cut me a bit of slack but I know a reverse-tail when I see one. There are three of them – big boys, young and broad with a bit of fun to them: the kind of fun that in childhood takes the heads off flies and in adulthood graduates to decapitating humans.

I break into a trot, hurrying into a lane where I remove my coat and sling it over my shoulder to mess with the profile, but the box is a dead giveaway so they're still with me when I reach Cleveland, laughing and joshing but still keeping pace as I head across the park to Central.

Once upon a time Prince Alfred Park was down-at-heel tennis courts, bedraggled trees and people sleeping off whatever people go to parks to sleep off. Then money got in the way and now it's got a fancy-pants swimming pool and acres of green grass infested with joggers playing tag with personal trainers. I head for the fence behind the oleanders. *When you want to hide something,* Rube always said, *put it where everyone can see it. And when you got something to protect, use it as a weapon.*

I sling the coat into the bushes, do the coffin-swing and get the first joker on the side of the toboggan with a sidekick from the whitesides, á la Nureyev. Then, using the box as a counterweight, I catch the second with a back-kick to the capellas. One to go. I put down the box and prance forward to meet him, arms out with fingers extended. Only to find he's no longer there. There's two thugs dancing on the path with all the grace of a pair of legless centipedes but the third one's vanished. I pick up the coffin without looking back which is a mistake because when I do I find that –

They've disappeared and with them my coat. And with the coat, Rube's *PRIVATE AND PERSONAL* file that I'd carefully sequestered in the inside pocket.

The boat's a fine and private place but none I think do there embrace. The *Wooden No* still rocks at its mooring and it's still in danger of sinking but I'm not feeling so good. *When you feel bad,* Rube said, *bury yourself in your work.* So I do like she said and bury myself in cases she's both solved and not solved over the years. *Correction:* I don't bury myself – I go through the cases methodical in the hope that I'll find what I'm looking for.

People's memories come to a grinding halt with accidents. One minute they're in the passenger seat chatting to the driver, the next they're in hospital with their neck in a brace and the driver's dead, and they can't remember a thing. A mobile phone rings but it's a long time before I answer. I know it's a long time because by the time I click on, the voice at the other end is up to the expletives.

'Jesus, Rainbow, I thought you were dead!'

Roarer's still caught up with his guilt, still trying to shift the blame. I click off. He calls back.

'Mate, I just need to know if you're still alive. I was going to call around and, you know …'

'Well, don't call around and you know.'

'I thought you might have a job for me.'

'Anything else?'

'Thingo copped it this afternoon.'

'Who's *thingo?*'

'I can't say over the phone because you'll only hang up. But you know because you've been expecting it. That's why you asked me to watch him. Well, when I went round he …'

Roarer's hard enough to understand at the best of times but through the filter of security he's an enigma tied up in a question mark wrapped in a tiger blanket. But I've worked out who *thingo* was. I only hope they didn't hurt him too much before they killed him.

'Also, I remembered the word,' he adds.

'What word?'

'The one that the other you-know-what said – the one starting with N.'

I take the risk because it's important.

'What was the word?'

'Indigo.'

'But *indigo* doesn't start with *N* ...'

'It does when you think about it.'

Chapter 15

US AND THEM

I stay away. They – *someone* – will be expecting me so instead I work through Rube's files. *Don't get caught up in detail,* I tell myself. *There isn't time.* The bottle's empty so I find myself a full one and start it on its way to emptiness. It means there'll be fire in the guts and foolishness in the brain but suddenly I'm in urgent need of both. First Rube then Harry – with Tsunami and the rest of them lined up waiting on the gangplank. Foolishness first ...

A phone rings. I find out which one from the selection in the bilge and click the thing on. The voice is like the whisky – still maturing. It's Bertie, the kid from Vaucluse.

'Have you discovered anything yet?'

Suddenly I'm sober. 'Yeah – I've discovered that these friends of yours mean business.'

'They're not friends and they're still after me.'

'Then you'll have to go into hiding. Work in an ashram in India or something.'

'I don't think Daddy would approve of that.'

It's Rube's computer and therefore dirty but at least it's traceable only to Rube and no-one can hurt her where she's gone. I open Gargle, come up with Bertie's email and – after a lot less than the usual trial and terror – find that his password is the same as his name. Also that – apart from the expected emails to friends and relations – there's nothing even faintly suspicious. Nothing, for example, linking him to terrorist groups like Hezbollah or al-Qaedar or Khalid Sheikh Mohammed or the deaths of Harry and Rube. After that I try *Father of* and after that chuck the computer in the water. I'm not as innocent as Bertie.

He's a name from Rube's files under the heading *Security Adviser*, he's big and he's wearing the kind of expression that a ghost might wear on his day off. I can't see through him – just where the bookshelves covering the back of his office stop on one side of his suit and come out the other. He's frowning over my card – the one that says I'm a vice-president of something or other in an obscure concern that might or might not be important.

'What did you say you were interested in?'

You don't need a fake moustache or a funny accent to change people's perceptions of you – just a change of clothes, a self-effacing manner and an all-purpose chuckle. I do the chuckle.

'Please don't take too much notice of the card, John – you don't mind if I call you John, do you?

If we can do business we'll do it and if we can't, we never met.'

He persists. They always persist. 'What kind of business are you in?'

'Security.'

'That's a big word, security.'

I keep my hands still – that's a large part of the secret, keeping your hands still – and look at him like he's a cross between Steve Irwin and the Dalai Lama.

'You're a shrewd man, John. And yes, security's a very big word, which is why I'm here. I'm not trying to sell you anything or even buy something from you. As a newcomer to your country, I simply need the answer to a question, and that question is: *Is Australia safe?*'

'Economically, politically or socially?'

I get the impression I'm looking in a mirror, that I'm as fake as this joker representing himself to me as a security adviser.

'That's a very clever question and of course the three are connected.' I do the chuckle. 'I guess what I'm saying is: should I invest here?'

'That's another big word, *invest*.'

He looks at his watch – he's got a couple of minutes, no more: it's time to cut to the chase.

'But neither *security* nor *invest* is the key word. The key word's *control*. And the answer to your question is, *Here in Australia, yes, we are in control.* Our two main political parties might represent themselves as Whig and Tory but in fact they're one and the same. Which makes us *safe* in every sense of the word.' He shoots me his Steve Lama look. 'So, yes, everything's under control.'

I find what I'm looking for towards the end of the second bottle, a thinner file than the rest because the case was incidental, worked on only when Rube had time and spread out over a number of years, starting when I was eight. The file's vague, no doubt intentionally so:

1. Because Rube hadn't had time to collect all the data; and

2. In case someone other than me found it.

It's called *THEM*, it contains no more than a few pages and those few pages contain nothing that could be called even vaguely coherent. *When doing a crossword,* Rube wrote, *you need to put yourself in the mind of the setter. That's the key, the clue, the thread — the code, if you like. You need to work out the compiler's mindset, see if they like anagrams or acrostics or spoonerisms or just mucking about with the mind of the solver. Because once you've worked out their mindset you have a chance of solving the crossword. Indigo,* Rory said. Rory who wouldn't know *indigo* from *impetigo* or a hole in the ground … I stare at the empty bottle. How come it's empty? A ferry rocks the *Wooden No* and the pump stops. I'm inclined to let it stay stopped but after a while I go down and get it started again.

The moonlight shining through the porthole's from the same moon that shone on the world when life began. Then it stops shining and the cabin's dark. The moon that's been shining forever has gone because the *Wooden No*'s swung on her mooring. *THEM*, the file's labelled. And in it is what Rube worked out over a number of years. Did it ever achieve the status of *Case*? Rube wrote beneath the heading: *Is this important?* To which there's no reply, just the same silence that's filling the cabin now – the plash of innocent wavelets against the hull and the tick of the old tub's chronometer marking off measured increments of time.

In the middle of the night, Roarer rings again.

'It might have been something else.'

'What might have been something else?'

'That word I told you – it might have been *in-he-go*.'

'Thanks for that, Roarer.'

'Don't mention it.' This time he's the one that clicks off.

Chapter 16

DIS IS DE NIECE

The café's so much charred wreckage ringed by the usual blue-and-white plastic tape. In the pallid light of the setting sun, the blackened benchtops are broken, plastic plates reduced to Dali shapes and the words chalked on the footpath read *NEVA X US*. It's been a fine day but not for Harry – his corpse is in the morgue and his home's in Cammeray.

I'm loitering on the other side of the road pretending to read the *Terrorgraph*. I don't know why they still produce the *Terrorgraph* – how many private eyes need a tabloid blatt to hide behind while waiting to gain entry to an apartment? Photos of the burnt-out caff accompany the story, together with a grainy head-and-shoulders of an old but very dead friend.

YET ANOTHER DEATH
CAFE MAN KILLED
When will this carnage end?
An old dame's having trouble getting out of the

block of flats because she's tangled in a walking frame so I help her before the security doors shut, keeping the gat closeted because there's no need for armoury – it would only frighten the pigeons. In the foyer there's the usual ragged carpet and peeling paint, the stairs creak and the smell alone could kill you.

Harry's door's open.

Inside the flat the carpet's heavily patterned, the walls were last painted fifty years ago and a woman's foot is dangling from an unmade bed. It's the stuff that mantraps are made of so I stay where I am. The building contains twenty bedsits with a lot of punters hanging around in the daytime because they got nowhere else to go. Above the muted roar of traffic there isn't a sound and the foot on the bed keeps swinging.

The trick to detective work is to stay out of range – be a fly on the wall instead of an active participant. But it doesn't always work that way. The door next to Harry's opens, a gorilla emerges and I make out I belong here, push Harry's door open all the way and find I'm no longer a fly on the wall – instead I'm in the middle of a tableau containing chintz curtains, a few scraps of furniture with Harry's stamp collection on one of the scraps, in the presence of the dame belonging to the foot.

She's in her early twenties and she's supporting her nicely distributed weight on one hand while she's got a gat in the hand she's not leaning on. The gun's a Para-Ordnance Warthog, a handy little number with a sharp-release hammer which makes it highly accurate – not a good thing if you're at the pointy end which is where I am. I wave my arms in the hope that it looks like I'm either a very close friend or surrendering.

'Don't shoot,' I plead.

'I won't,' the dame replies. 'At least not yet.'

Her black hair's done tousled, her face is pale, her eyes are minus the epicanthic fold and she's wearing a loose dress without much support to it – but who needs support when you're holding a Warthog? Her foot's still making like a metronome and her expression's somewhere between suspicious and suspicious. After a while her foot stops swinging, her lips tighten and I decide against jumping her. The gun's too steady and the gaze hasn't wavered from my sternum.

'I've been waiting for you,' she murmurs.

'There must be some mistake.'

'Yes, there must, mustn't there?'

I could stand here forever swapping pleasantries only I haven't got forever. I came to look for clues – apart from the expected ones – only to be confronted by the totally *un*expected ones.

'You're either Harry's niece or his daughter. One thing's for sure – you ain't his mother.'

The dame laughs. At least I think she's laughing because the almond eyes crease and the mouth twitches like there's a fly on it but the gat doesn't move so maybe I'm wrong.

'That's two shots, mister, both of them wide of the mark.'

'That's too bad,' I reply, 'because I've already decided you were an interloper which is why I called the cops.'

That's when her eyes waver and that's when I take her. A ballet move always fools them. Instead of diving, I do the splits. Then instead of staying split I do the kind of roll Margot Fontaine would have been proud of, followed by a grab of the metronome foot and a twist that puts the dame on the floor a millisecond too fast for her to reorganise the gun. I relieve her of the firepower, get to my feet, close the door and switch on the light. And with the light on I rebadge her. She's small, aged twenty-five going on fifteen and the lips in the Hepburn face – that's Audrey not Katharine – are set in a snarl that stops a millimetre short of beautiful. She's about to speak but I get in first.

'So what's it to be – *sister, niece* or *daughter*?'

'I was Harry's girlfriend,' she says, a sad expression clouding her face.

'You got a name, girlfriend?'

'Yes, I do,' she says.

'Mind telling me what it is?'

'Yes, but I'll tell you anyway – it's Denise.' She smiles at a memory. 'Harry always introduced me to people as *de niece* but to my face it was always *Babychino*.' She glances at me shyly or maybe it's slyly – it's hard to tell because of the eyes. 'I know who you are – you're Rainbow.'

'Where were you at the time of Harry's death?'

She doesn't miss a beat, segueing from grief to reliable eyewitness in less than an eye-bat.

'I was going to meet him,' she says straight from the hip, 'but by the time I arrived it was all over. Harry was in a bad way but he still managed to say something.'

'What did he say?'

'He said: *Life is only froth and bubble.*'

'Did that mean anything to you?'

She nods before answering. 'It meant that he recognised me even though he was dying. I used to – I still do – shoot off at the mouth. And when that happened Harry said I was living up to my name of Babychino: frothy. Then he'd mess with this quote and say: *Life is only froth and bubble/Two things stand like stone/Blindness to another's trouble/Cunning in your own.*'

'When did he say that?'

'All the time. But he didn't really mean it.'

'Is that all?'

'Isn't it enough?'

Chapter 17

THE BIG BOY

'It depends whether I prefer milk with my coffee or like it straight. Going back a couple of stanzas, Bubbles – you said you were hurrying. Why?'

'Because –' Babychino glances away '– Harry was under threat.'

'Who was he under threat from? Debt dealers? Junkies? Standover men after his property?'

Babychino moves to the door where she pauses with her hand on the handle but her mind elsewhere.

'After you and that woman rode off on the scooter, the terrorists came back the the café, wanting to know where you lived. Harry wouldn't tell them. There were too many people around for them to do anything but they threatened to return.'

'Where were you when he copped it?'

'I told you – I was on my way to see him.' She's got her composure back from wherever she parked it and she's tugging at the curtains, moving furniture, adjusting bedcovers – all the things a person does who's familiar with a joint – pausing only long enough to add, 'This was our love nest.'

'When did the cops arrive?'

'While I was kneeling beside Harry.'

'Were they real cops?'

'What kind of question's that?'

'Did they ask who you were?'

'Yes.'

'What did you tell them?'

'I told them we were lovers.'

I think back to Aunt Rube.

'Did they invite you to do an official ID?'

'Yes.'

'What did you tell them?'

'I confirmed it was him.'

'Why did you call them *terrorists*?'

'Because that's what they must have been.'

'Did the cops ask you about any identifying marks?'

'Yes.'

'Did you show them the birthmark in the shape of a boat on his right ankle?' I say it quick so there's no time for evasion.

'It wasn't a birthmark, it was a scar; it wasn't on his right ankle, it was on his left side; and it wasn't a boat, it was a bird.' She gives me one of her glances. 'Do I pass?' She shivers. 'It's like reliving it all over again. But they say you have to relive things if you're going to cope.'

It seems like Harry had good taste in everything except what he dished up to his customers.

They've cemented over the dirt, the gym's been turned into a theatre and the demountables have been replaced with permanent classrooms. A sign reads *BE NICE TO YOUR NEIGHBOURS* while a second one warns students to *REPORT UNUSUAL ACTIVITY.* It's Sunday, so the school's deserted, but I people it with savages.

When I was a kid, if you reported 'unusual activity' you became part of the unusual activity. Like Harry, I had a girlfriend – or what passes for a girlfriend when you're ten. I even remember her name and what she looked like. The corrugated-iron toilets have been rebuilt in expensive new brick and the gallows tree's still standing except that now it's fenced off with *STRICTLY OUT OF BOUNDS* signs hanging from its branches. I climb over the fence.

I need faces, shapes, bodies and attitudes to go with the names that I haven't got and they swarm all over me. The footholes are still in the trunk and I can still hear the shouts and feel the hands dragging me through the foliage. The marks of the rope have filled with lichen but they're still there and the bloodlust echoes through time.

I crawl out on the branch. Rube calls it – make that *called* it – *method detecting.* I see the chanting kids like they're still there, feel the tightening of the rope and – just before passing out – the anxious face of Ariadne Indola behind the willow-switch form of the Headmaster as he hurries towards us, waving a pair of scissors and shouting, *You little brat, why are you doing this to me?*

I pleaded with Rube not to make a fuss. But

after she was satisfied I was okay, she visited the Headmaster. He was on the defensive – he'd saved her brat, who'd brought it on himself by not mixing more easily with the others. *Be assured,* he told her, *the ringleaders will be expelled.* Rube was aghast. *Can't you see what that will do?* she replied. *They'll come after him!*

Back aboard the *Wooden No*, I crack a bottle of J&B and continue sifting through Rube's files. Despite what she told the Headmaster, she thought it was just Darlinghurt being Darlinghurt and it took her a while to figure out what was really going on. She set traps, caught some of the transgressors, gave them a kick up the bum and life returned to more-or-less normal. Then – years down the track – the persecution started again. Only this time it was more like drip torture – subtle, not so easy to pin down. Whispers in the crowd, items missing from the house, nasty little notes in the mail. All of which Rube took in her stride because she'd lived with such things all her life. It wasn't until she put two and two together that she started the dossier.

Something happened to make it start all over again but it's not clear what. I find nothing in Rube's files apart from the single question: *Why?* Apart from which, I never noticed anything and people change. All I remember is that the ringleader was a big boy. Somehow Rube came by the names, only I let them get stolen before I had the chance to commit them to memory.

A ferry passes, the *Wooden No* rocks and the empty bottles roll with her. By nightfall I'm rolling with the boat because I'm as drunk as a day-old newt. A ship's hooter bleats and over a distance of thirty-five years all I've got is a fistful of six-by-four-inch cards, each containing little more than nothing – a few vague references to a bunch of bully boys, one of them – the ringleader – big.

I don't do vengeance; this isn't a vendetta. Rube's dead and nothing I can do will bring her back. I stare at the screen. The figures on the CCTV weren't middle-aged like they should be – middle-aged men move careful and at least one of them would be stiff-backed with care. How can I find out, how can I *know*? Rube knew – which was why she went to the trouble of keeping records. It's also why they came after her. So surely –

Chapter 18

LOOKING FOR ARIADNE

Something whangs against the hull and nausea assails me as I ease myself up from my bunk, assume an approximation of the perpendicular and stagger out on deck. A fish flops at my feet.

'Ahoy there, me hearty!'

Queen the Sailorman's strutting around the stern of his boat wearing Gucci. Breakfast is flathead. I try to stare him down but can't because of his bonhomie and the sun. There's a time for everything and this isn't one of them. I toe the fish back in the water.

'Sixteen men on a dead man's chest!' he sings as he throttles away; someone ought to throttle Queen. 'Yo, ho, ho, and a bottle of Calvados! Row, row, row the boat! Sixteen men ...'

The echoes recede as I crawl back to my bunk. *Sixteen men,* Queen's singing. I can't remember sixteen men – make that *boys;* I can't even remember one.

What do you know when you're a kid? You know how to survive and after that you know what you like and what you don't like and you do something about it. And what I did – at least once every schoolday – was I held Ariadne Indola's hand. The one and only thing I hated about my deschooling was that it meant leaving behind the girl of my dreams.

On the computer at the internet café, for plain and unadorned *Indola* I get the infernal question: *Do you mean Indolent?* But as well as the question, I also get a couple of *Indolas* – namely *George, Simon* and *Marguerita*. Even after I apply the acid test – *parents of* – I still come up empty-handed. Around me, kids watch porn and social misfits harass other social misfits. A virtual life is no life at all and I can't find Ariadne.

Because the machine is logical, the computer asks: *Do you mean Indole, Indolo or India.* I try what they suggest followed by a few things completely different. Then I insert a couple of asterisks. Finally, *Bingo!* There's the name change – to *Indox* – while the first name remains the same. The girl of my dreams is still Ariadne – the only offspring of a couple that was once Indola but somewhere along the line changed their name, for reasons best known to themselves.

They supported polar bears in Alaska, muskrats in the Ukraine, set up a fighting fund to stop oil mining in the North Sea and sent their only child into the jaws of death – namely Baisson Primary – in accordance with their principles regarding equal education for all. But I already know that because, apart from holding hands, me and Ariadne Indola also talked. What I don't know is what she died of. Because Ariadne Indox – née Indola – apparently no longer exists.

Until I scroll to the end of all the good deeds of the Indolas – make that *Indoxes* – to discover that she does.

The joint's one of those pleasantries that God inducted and Man constructed – a tower of ice-cold marble with forty floors of pastel-tinted windows smiling back at the sun. The foyer's an introduction to infamy and there's a thug standing guard.

'What do you want?' he snarls.

Not *How can I help you, my good man?* Or *Good morning, sir, isn't it a nice day?*

'I'm a friend of Merz Sidonia's.'

He doesn't even make the call, just comes at me like a loaded howitzer. You don't negotiate with loaded howitzers so I thump him. Blame an imbalance of derivatives.

Money does people's dirty work for them. Here it locks down the building, sounds an alarm and calls in the heavy artillery. Before I can hit *Rewind* I find myself cross-stitched to a chair in a small room undergoing the kind of interrogation that can only result in a great deal of pain.

'The police will be here in –' The security boss stretches his long legs under the desk and consults his imitation Rolex '– twenty minutes and fifteen seconds. They always allow us a bit of leeway.' With his grey eyes he could be a film star with a bank account in the Bahamas. 'During that leeway, we have free rein to do anything we like, short of killing you.'

He's got my gat on his desk and he's studying it, along with the contents of my pockets.

I try again. 'Like I said, I'm a friend of Merz Sidonia's.'

'And I'm the King of Siam.' He assumes a smile about as real as his watch. 'I suppose you're going to tell me you're here to give her the gun?'

'The gat's no more than part of the wardrobe, a fashion accessory that means nothing and does even less. I'm here to see Ariadne.'

The security boss puts down the Smith & Double-Yew, raises his eyes to mine and suddenly they're not so much grey as overcast and threatening.

'The point is –' he checks the calling cards that he filched along with the gat '– Mr Green or Orange or whatever you're calling yourself today – you can't see anyone. How do we know who you are? You come here armed to your broken teeth and when you find entry difficult, knock out my concierge. Which means you've just bought yourself a one-way ticket to the cop shop – and after that court, followed by jail. Unless you can come up with a far more convincing explanation for your visit than the one provided.'

That's when she appears. Ariadne was only a girl when I last saw her, with shiny hair, big opossum eyes and skin like caramel ice-cream. A hand you needed to hold and a smile that lit up your life. Thirty-five years later I'm strapped to a chair and not in a position to disbelieve anything. But what I see puts a lump in my throat. Thirty-five years after my last sighting, my lovely little girlfriend advances into the room.

'It's not – it couldn't be … Rainbow?'

Since the age of consent I've been supporting the whisky business and last night was no exception. I've had my ears mashed and my nose broken and the cut over my right eye gives me a permanent expression of malevolent quizzicality. Add to that the missing thumb, too much musculature and the op-shop wardrobe and – like they say in the classics – I leave a lot not to be desired.

'One and the same. Except that – like you – I'm all growed up now.'

Ariadne walks to where the sunlight can pick up any imperfections she's collected over thirty-five years. Gone is the little white dress, to be replaced by a sheer-silk number in iridescent mauve, reaching sedately below her knees and covering most of her shoulders but having difficulty covering subsequent developments. Of course she's taller. Otherwise she is as she always was, just older.

'Make that,' I add, '*not* just like you.'

Chapter 19

THE GIRL OF MY DREAMS

I manage to grind the thug's foot into the marble before following Ariadne into her private Otis elevator and halfway to heaven. You meet someone out of the mockery of the past but you don't see them – what you see instead is yourself as they see you. And what I see through Ariadne's eyes as she seats herself behind a desk big enough to waltz on is a gaudily dressed pug with a face hacked out of misfortune, twisting a battered hat in his ham fists, and shifting from one foot to the other like he needs to go to the toilet.

'Remember when we used to hold hands?' I say. 'Except you'd always let go when that bully-boy appeared, I suppose in case he hurt me for consorting with you.'

'I remember.'

'Do you also remember the one about the three wells?'

'Well, well, well …' she murmurs, smiling at the memory of what used to make us laugh while I try to get used to an office big enough to double as a launch-pad for an Airbus. The bank of telephones before her is a private army and the view from the window is pretty much what Gurgle Earth would get from a satellite. I turn back to Ariadne – you can only get so far on satellites.

'Speaking of *well,*' I say, 'you look great.'

She shrugs. 'Mum and Dad looked like teenagers well into their sixties; I didn't have children; I'm cushioned by wealth; on top of which I keep fit by stroking in a women's rowing team. All I need to worry about are taxes and the Troubles and neither is going to prematurely age me because I've got everything covered.'

Because I'm a detective, like the character in the Notre Dame book I get hunches. And my hunch right now is that – apart from finding out the present-day identity of the boy that used to bully me – those *Troubles* might be worth knowing.

'What Troubles might they be?'

She smooths her hands over her arms like she might be able to iron out perfection.

'As I said, they're nothing I can't handle. In fact I only really became aware of them after James died' – she waves a beautiful arm at the desk, the launchpad and the view – 'leaving me this.'

'Could you be a bit more specific?'

She shakes her beautiful head. 'What are you?' she asks. 'Oh, I know you *used* to be Rainbow but what have you become? You might be from the Tax Office or one of those TV shows that do exposés or from a spy agency or the police. Having all those business cards suggests you might be far more than you appear to be. I know *who* you are – what I don't know is *what.*'

'I'm a private detective.'

'And are you here to investigate my business or me?'

I shake my head to indicate reassurance but in reality to stop my mind buzzing. I'm interested in who she remembered from school only to be sidetracked by talk of the Troubles and her beauty.

'I'm here for something else entirely.'

'How do I know that?'

'Because I came in by the front door.'

She plays with the little replicas of trucks, scale models of edifices, bundles of share scrip and gold ingots that litter her desk and when she looks up she's come to a decision.

'I'm sorry if I seem suspicious, Rainbow – it's the nature of business that people are out to get you. It's one way of winning – by hobbling the opposition. I wasn't brought up to money or I'd never have been at that school. As a late convert to wealth I tend to be over-protective of it. But I trust you because of our past so I'll do my best to help. What do you want to know?'

'We could start with the Troubles ...'

She puts down a model of a dredger. 'Not to put too fine a point on it, James – that's my late husband – was paranoid. He thought there were two threats facing business – one from within and one from without: traditional workplace problems that have always been there plus a new one – which, for want of a better word, he called *terrorism*. It was the latter he was most worried about. So he set up a department to study what he perceived to be a very great threat, thereby providing himself with the wherewithal to deal with it. He called his department *Watchdog*. At the time, I didn't know the background or what he did with the information.'

She looks across her airfield desk to see if she's got my attention; she has.

'I use the word *paranoid* but it seems that there *was* something to my husband's fears. Among other things we dabble in coal-seam gas and it was assumed that a series of disasters was the work of eco-terrorists – that is, well-intentioned do-gooders we could bundle off to court and be rid of, relying on our PR people to stop us looking like bullies. But Watchdog found there was more than that. Which is how we became mixed up in politics –' She stops like she's just remembered something. 'But enough of my problems – what happened to you?'

'After those bullies nearly killed me?' I shrug myself into a chair. 'Against my will – I was only a kid, remember – my Aunt Rube took me out of school. She was my sole care and consolation.'

'You talk as if she's –'

'Dead? Yeah, that's why I'm here. Rube taught me to be a detective and that's what I became. I'm looking for her killer – or killers.'

'Who do you think killed her?'

'I don't know. It could have been the kids from school, the ones that nearly hanged me, evolved from schoolboy bullies into murderers. It might be someone else entirely. Or it might be your terrorists.'

When Ariadne's smile fades, the lights go out. She picks up a little clock and taps it like she wants to stop time.

'You do know, don't you, that your incident with

the bullies was my epiphany? I don't mean I had a vision but afterwards my life changed. Because up to that time my parents wanted to bring me up according to their lights, which meant keeping me at that school.' She glances across the tarmac at me. 'Is this too much of a side-bend?'

'There's this theory doing the rounds that everything's connected,' I say. 'So go on.'

'Although my parents were moderately wealthy, they sent me to Baisson Primary because of their beliefs, even though it had to be the worst school in Sydney. But after the incident in the playground there was no way their precious Ariadne was going to swing for their principles so they took me out, changed their name to Indox and fast-tracked me through the kind of education that led to finishing school and ultimately marriage to a rich old man.' A wave of her hand takes in the room and the view and ends up with me. 'While it appears that you –'

Chapter 20

KICK PRO QUO

I shrug.

'Yeah, I went to *unfinishing* school and ended up going in the opposite direction.' I clamber to my feet. 'I won't take up any more of your precious time, Ariadne. I just thought you might be able to help.'

'Is this some kind of vendetta?'

I shake my head. 'Someone killed my Aunt Rube and I thought it might have been the kids from school with *their* vendetta. No, it's not a vendetta because I don't do vendettas. I just thought that, because you knew those bullies, you might also know where I could find them.'

She takes her eyes off the clock.

'I can't help you with any of that. But as I said, I have friends in positions of power. You can read it in any newspaper but as it happens I donate. And the people I donate to have much the same interests as my business does. They want employment – we give them employment. They want income from workers' taxes – we give them such income. And they're as concerned about terrorism as we are. From what you say, the death of your aunt might be the work of terrorists. And while I don't know any of your bullies, I do have political contacts who might be able to help.'

She writes something on a scrap of paper. As if acting on impulse, because that's the way it plays, I come around the desk to show that I still harbour some feelings towards her. But she's too quick and presses a button under her desk. There's a knock at the door and without waiting for an answer the thug enters, like he's more than anxious to take up where he left off.

'Yes, Miss Ariadne?' he asks.

'Our visitor's just leaving.'

I plant a kiss on her cheek – it seems called for – and in return she hands me the scrap of paper.

'I'm sorry I can't be more helpful,' she says. 'But if you think of some way in which I might be, please don't hesitate to call. Our Headmaster's name, by the way, was Jonathan Hercule.'

Visiting Ariadne was a long shot and, in the way of long shots, all it's left me with is memories. I'm still no closer to finding Rube's killers. Added to which is the fact that I'm wondering how things might have been if I'd stayed at school and faced the music – even if the lyrics didn't say *murder boys* but *gird her loins*. But like Rube said: *Might have been – schmite have been: what didn't happen can never be regretted. All you have after the past is the here and now. Unless, of course, something happens to change it – like the future.*

Irving Morris is a big man in his bitter middle years who looks like he might know a lot more than he does. We're in the headquarters of some political party and the office looks like it could double as a storeroom. I let him make the play.

'This isn't my room. Mrs Sidonia didn't say *who* you were nor did she say *what* you wanted to see me about. Besides which, what would I know?'

It's a good question but I go through the motions anyway.

'Why would she direct me here if she didn't think you could help?'

'Would you like a cup of tea, Mr, er –'

'Brown – Terence Brown. You wouldn't have anything a bit stronger, would you?'

No, Morris says, and even if he did he wouldn't know where to find it because – as he's already pointed out – this isn't his room: someone far more powerful than he is lent it to him.

'Can I speak frankly, Mr – er – Brown?'

'Is there any other way?'

'Mrs Sidonia told me that your visit had to do with that anti-terrorist department of hers, a department that reminds me of those signs saying green for safe, amber for maybe and red for high fire danger. Her department happens to be remarkably similar to the one I head up for the party – as a matter of fact we work hand in glove. According to Mrs Sidonia – and I don't think she'd mind my saying this – Australia's going through a period of high fire danger. It's like global warming – no-one will admit it doesn't exist because it would disaffect too many voters. But society has to be kept safe. And that department of hers, in lockstep with mine, helps keep society safe. Do I make myself clear?'

It's like a secret handshake. And while he's using the kind of code these people use I've got an idea I know what he's saying and I've also got an idea I don't like it – the crazy, red-eyed view of politics where the secret of life is to make a lot of money and if anyone gets in your way, kick them in the teeth so they don't do it again. I terminate the interview.

After my meeting with Genghis Khan, I need a breath of fresh air so I telephone Imogene. She might be learning how to be a cop but that doesn't mean she's not still my daughter. It's easy to reach her now she's no longer living with my ex-wife, her mother.

'Hello, darling? I'm ringing from a phonebooth that somehow still works which means there's no chance of a bug – from my end, anyway. What about yours?'

My ebullience is met with silence. Maybe I could have been more tactful, tactical, played it as it lays. I try again.

'I just rang for a chat, Chickadee. How are you?'

'I can't talk just now, Daddy, I'm in a lecture. But while you're there, could I ask a favour? Could you not call me so often? It makes life *difficult*. They give us heaps of homework and also there are lectures, tutorials, PE, drill and as well as that I ...'

'It's okay, Chickadee. Goodbye.'

'Goodbye, Daddy.'

I've put a lot of coins in the slot in anticipation of a long call but there's still a lot left after I hang up. I hit *Return* but nothing comes out. Faulty phone.

Chapter 21

CRUSHED BONES

Jonathan Hercule's wearing a moth-eaten pink cardigan and his spectacles are growing out of the top of his head like an afterthought.

'Are you calling on behalf of a charity, did I win the Lotto or are you here to assassinate me to get your hands on the tinful of out-of-date banknotes under my bed?' He peers at me; his breath smells of dirty socks. 'You look familiar.'

I'm standing on a concrete verandah belonging to a block of flats that could double as a high-security prison.

'I was one of your students at Baisson Primary.'

'Which one were you?'

'The quiet one.'

The head on the end of the long neck bobs until it looks like it could fall off.

'I remember – you were the boy who was always being bullied. Caused me no end of trouble. You had an aunt.'

'What do you mean – *had*?' It's the chance he's been waiting for.

'My tense was preterite rather than pluperfect.

That is, while I knew you *had* an aunt then, I do not know if you still possess one *now*. The tense employed does not presume the demise of your aunt.'

'As it happens my aunt *is* dead, which is why I'm here.' Searching the darkness behind him is like trying to see into the past. 'Mind if I come in?'

I follow him into room that, if it was any bigger, would qualify as a sarcophagus. A plate edged in yellow was lunch and gunshots are rattling from the television. The old man fumbles a pointer and the gunshots cease.

'I don't normally watch television,' he says. 'But because it was about religion I made an exception. I was just about to have a cuppa – would you care to join me, ah … what did you say your name was?'

'The name's Rainbow.' I'm at school again and I don't want to be at school again. 'And I'm here to find out what you remember.'

My ex-Headmaster spoons too much tea into a teapot the size of a thimble – most of it goes on the floor – before adding water, most of which goes the same way as the tea.

'Next to nothing, I'm afraid. A lifetime spent trying to educate numbskulls like you tends to drain one – sometimes I even have trouble remembering where I put my glasses.' He hands me a cup I can see through. 'But I'm still a teacher – which is why I provide the following information: the material your cup's made from is called bone china because it's made from crushed bones.'

'Something like blood oranges.'

'It's not at all like blood oranges.' There's a frown

but it clears; he's been around kids all his life and is up to their tricks, even when they're not tricks. 'It's nice of you to drop by, if only to ask questions.'

'I'm not nice and neither are my questions. Do you remember a hanging?'

'Is this a joke? Are you trick-or-treating? Has that infernal pumpkin time come around again?'

'It happened in the schoolyard – a girl called Ariadne went and got you and you ran to my assistance. You were carrying scissors.'

He frowns into his bone cup, staring at the worn carpet, then looks at me as though through a cottonwool shroud.

'If what you say is true I shouldn't have done that – run with scissors. It sets a bad example. I've expelled students for less.'

'Like you expelled that boy over the hanging.'

'You should have said: "*As* you expelled that boy over the hanging". *Like* is used to introduce a simile – but you wouldn't know a simile if you tripped over one on a night as dark as ashes.' He shakes his head like – as though – he wants to rid himself of the cottonwool but can't. 'What hanging?'

'My hanging. I was hung. From a tree.'

'*Hanged.*' The correction's automatic. 'Pictures are hung, people are hanged. Didn't you learn anything?'

'What was his name?'

'Whose?'

'The boy you expelled.'

After a pause, he says, 'I believe it was Parkinson. He used to sit up the back and tease the girls.' He looks confused. 'But why would he try to hang you?

And what tree?'

I turn to go. 'It's *which* tree. And if you're looking for your glasses they're on top of your head.'

In 1930s Chicago, speakeasies were outlets for hooch – illegal grog distilled by sweatshops called *alky-burners* and distributed by gangsters like Al Capone. But the prohibited substances of today wear names like crack, ice and gammahydroxybutyrate – fantasy or liquid ecstasy – shortened to *GHB* because its users can't manage to say more than one syllable at a time. And because the drugs are illicit, speakeasies like O'Leary's pull in starlets looking for excitement, common-and-garden addicts, plenty of cops and Sydney's usual crop of colourful identities. Roarer's propping up the bar.

'I'm getting screwed,' he says. 'It's like prostitution after they brought in free love – us professionals lose out to over-enthusiastic amateurs. I ask you, where's the justice?'

Hank the barman hands me a Pink Whizz with a maraschino cherry in it and a smile.

'Justice is where it's always been, Roarer – under the jewel-encrusted jockstrap of the nearest politician. When will you learn that it simply isn't for people like us? It's to safeguard the rich and powerful which is the reason why it was invented in the first place. There's nothing you can do about it so have another beer.'

Roarer hunches over his hooch. All he knows

is that his missus left him, after which he left the Church, which leaves him free to go back to killing.

'It's a bastard about Harry – he never hurt anyone, except when they deserved it. Got another job for me? I can do toecaps, kneecaps or the single shot to the back of the head for no better reason than someone smiled at someone else's missus. I don't charge GST and there's only a slight adjustment for inflation. Cash on the knocker – or should I say *knock*.'

After leaving Hercule I got to work on the White Pages and found too many subscribers with the surname Parkinson. But upon inquiry, most were the wrong age, two were dead and several belonged to the wrong sex. But one in Manly filled the bill: *Parkinson, T.F.* It might be him or it might just be an innocent bystander.

'Yeah, I got a job. Only it doesn't involve killing.'

'What *does* it involve?'

'Finding out who someone is, what they do and who they consort with.'

'A yawn job in other words. Are you sure you don't want them dead?'

I think of Rube and Harry. Sure I want them dead – only it's not what I do.

'It's not what I want, Roarer. It's what's got to be done.'

Chapter 22

THE WOMAN IN RED

We're battling the *elephants* along Manly's Corso, the parade within a parade without a single bikini in sight, looking for an address spat out by a computer. Sydney's having a weather moment, the kind when Scotsmen wish they'd worn underpants. The wind could sink the *Wooden No* but I haven't got time to worry about boats. I got my hands full with Rory.

'You sure it's just a watch-and-wait job? Because if not, my crutch is loaded and ready to go and …'

'Like I said, Roarer, this ain't a death job.'

Most of my words are blown away before they reach him and I don't know which words but it doesn't matter because I've just seen the shadow that followed us onto the ferry and is still there – a black shape, lithe and dangerous-looking, flitting between buildings. It could be a garbage bag blown by the wind – if the wind wasn't going in the opposite direction. I drag Rory into a piece of prime real estate labelled *MENS*.

'Our target lives in that block of flats across the road, the one with the balconies,' I tell him. 'You'll enter by the usual means – that is, by holding the door open for an old lady and, while she's turning herself inside out saying *Thank you,* you go in. You'll make your way to his floor – the unit number will be on a letter box in the foyer alongside the name Parkinson.' I check my watch. 'By my calculation, you won't have to wait long. And remember, no shooting – you're only here to observe.'

'Observe what?'

'His salient features.'

'His *what?*'

It's like briefing a cistern.

'What he *looks* like, Roarer – his build and facial characteristics, his *appearance*. Got your mobile?'

'You want me to call him?'

It's not like there's a glut in the job market but surveillance is a niche industry and however the economy's doing you got to be happy with what you can get.

'Repeat after me, Roarer: you got your mobile – right?'

'Check.'

'Subject will appear at door of said apartment.'

'Check.'

'You'll photograph him and text me the image.'

'Isn't that insecure?'

'I'm insecure, you're insecure, the whole world's insecure. But my phone's traceable only to the morgue and I'd say the same thing applies to yours.'

'It's prepaid in someone else's name, if that's what you mean – what they call a *burner*, because after you've finished with it –'

'I know what a burner is, Roarer – it's what I'll turn on you if you blow it.'

The Manhattan began life as the tallest building in town but that was way back in the sixties. There are bigger buildings now but the Manhattan's still the one with the prestige – more pot plants per floor and a concierge that pre-revolutionary France would have been proud of. I'm wearing overalls with *PREMIER PLUMBING* on the bib and carrying the kind of attaché case a plumber takes to the most prestigious address in Sydney, if he wants to be invited back.

'Foul weather, friend,' the concierge says as he lets me in. 'And you're –?'

I point at the bib. 'Premier Plumbing. I'm expected upstairs.'

He hands me a card with a pin through it reading VISITOR. 'You'll need to wear this. Also I'll need some form of ID.' I give him the fake passport I used in the *Bullets at the Ballet* caper, the one featuring me as a baldy, a pilgarlic. 'Hair today, gone yesterday,' he says and I laugh because he expects me to while explaining I was never really bald, it just looks that way due to the stocking over my face, and he's still chuckling as he escorts me to the lift.

The first rule when you're somewhere you shouldn't be is to avoid the cameras. I exit the lift and step into the Gents just as Roarer's images arrive on my phone.

It's not him. That's my first thought as I study the snaps under a sign above the gold-plated taps. The man with the beard's big but he's too young. It could have been the wrong address, Roarer could have gone to the wrong door or it mightn't be the right Parkinson. I climb out of the overalls, jam on my fedora, stuff the overalls in my case, decant myself from the Gents and head for Suite 66.

'I'm from Ace Security,' I tell the receptionist, handing her the card that says I'm from Ace Security. 'We're doing a random check to make sure everything's in order, security-wise.' I keep my head down under the hat and hold up my all-purpose attaché case to prove I'm who I say I am. 'I'm looking for the office of a –' I pretend to check '– Thomas Parkinson.'

'I'm afraid Mr Parkinson's not in yet,' the receptionist says, smiling the smile of the bored while I nod the nod of a man who knows Mr Parkinson isn't in yet.

'When do you expect him?'

She glances at a clock on the wall. 'In ten minutes – exactly.'

'Is Mr Parkinson reliable?'

'You could set your clock by him.'

'Then I'll be all done and dusted in nine minutes – exactly.'

Rube taught me how to look like I'm doing one thing while doing another. Keeping the hat well down over my eyes I pull on the gloves, carry a chair to the corner and unfocus the camera while appearing to check it – five minutes. After that,

I make great play of patting down the office – checking bookshelves, running my hands under the desk, picking up the receiver of each of the three phones like I'm inspecting them, while all the time doing something completely different, which is checking the contents of the drawers. Five of which yield little or nothing while the sixth … I keep my eye on the time – six minutes.

When you steal anything, always leave room for doubt – take the money but leave the jewellery. The sixth drawer contains a small black notebook and wads of cash. I pocket the book, leave the cash and relock the drawer – all the while looking like I'm nowhere near it. Seven minutes. I snap a shot of the photo on the desk. Eight minutes. Nod to receptionist on way out – nine minutes.

Right on the ten-minute mark – after a trip to the Gents, I'm back in the plumber's overalls – he exits the lift accompanied by a woman in red and for a nanosecond the joker ceases to exist. She's blonde, her legs are straight off the lathe and the red frock clings to her like a rejected lover. Looks like a red herring.

'But darling,' she's saying to the man beside her, 'isn't that too high a price to pay for innocence?'

'No price is too high if you want something badly enough …'

He stops, frowning at the figure before him in the overalls.

'Your plumbing's fine,' I tell him.

It's nice to see the Woman in Red's cheeks dimple.

But she still looks like a red herring.

Chapter 23

THE CLUE

It's stopped raining and Rory's got his wet-weather gear strapped to the crutch that isn't a gun while using the other crutch to keep him upright. The roadway's glistening like shot velvet as we head down Macquarie Street towards the semi-circular quay.

'Spot-check time, Roarer. You went to the fifth floor, right?'

'Check – fifth floor.'

'And you waited outside the flat with your mobile up to your face like you were talking into it.'

'Check.'

'And the geezer came out of Flat 524.'

'Don't try to trick me, Rain.'

'Okay, 514 then. And he had a dame with him.'

'You didn't ask for a shot of the dame.'

'Just because I didn't ask …' A thought strikes me. 'Describe her.'

'Dumpy, dowdy and frowzy.'

Which means I got a case within a case within a dilemma because, like the Bard said, *Post hoc, ergo propter hoc* – a presumed cause might be an effect but usually isn't. Because when a lark appears, it doesn't mean it's summer – the sun might have come out anyway.

As we board the *Wooden No*, Queen yells a greeting. 'Ahoy, me hearty!'

'What do we do now?' asks Rory, climbing aboard after me.

'Kill Queen,' I reply. 'After which we go into deep surveill.'

After Roarer decamps and Queen ferries him back to the wharf, I check the little black book I filched from Parkinson. It's one of those diaries that isn't: from random notes on what the cat ate for dinner to a brand new recipe for bratwurst. I chuck it overboard and check the mobile pic of the desk photo. Beard, accompanied by dowdy wife. No sign of a dame in red or anyone else for that matter. He's a happily married man with no antecedents. I check an image from Rube's CCTV against Rory's shot of Parkinson and the one from the desk, freezing the frame when I get all three together.

There are no features on the CCTV because the faces are squashed under stockings and the image isn't all that crash-hot because the figures are moving. *There's something in the way they move.* I shuffle the images of Parkinson emerging from his flat and the snap from his desk with the still from the CCTV. No relation. Even under the stocking I'd notice the beard. I try the next image, followed by the next and the next. Still nothing – apart from suspicion.

Crime-scene tape's stretched across the pavement outside Rube's, the door's nailed back into position and there are too many gawkers. I avoid looking anyone in the eye as I make my way round the back. The kitchen stinks of mould and the hall's still redolent of eau de cologne.

I check the lounge where nothing's changed and the hall *ditto*. After which I head upstairs, fighting off the memory of Rube's body as I dust and photograph and dust and photograph some more. I take the group photo in the hall upstairs out of its frame and pocket it. The CCTV told me nothing and the relevant file's gone. All I've got is a name, a blurred photograph and Rube's thoughts. The bathroom cabinet contains pretty much what I expected – Rube was never the lipstick-and-scent type.

I could be on the wrong track entirely. Who says it's the gang from school or derivatives thereof? And why can't it be terrorists? Why does everything need to be what it appears *not* to be? Rube's Lesson No. 34: *You have induction, deduction and abduction – if one doesn't work, try one of the others.* Inducting from that: *Why shouldn't it be simple, straightforward, common-and-garden terrorism?*

I used to consult Harry but Harry's dead. Failing Harry there was always Rube but she's dead, too. Asking Rory would be like asking why dogs scratch themselves – he'd only come up with something like: *Why limit the question to dogs?* My old flame Annie might as well be on the other side of the moon, I split with Tsunami before anything started and Imogene's studying to become a cop. Which leaves just one person.

'I'll make coffee.'

I watch her move to the corner of the room. She told me to get in touch if I needed help and I need help. We dined on pie and peas at Jake's Café de Wheels in Woolly-Moo-Loo and afterwards made poetry out of the clouds and talked about old times.

'I learnt a lot,' Ariadne says.

'So did I – I learnt that people like to hurt people.'

'Not everyone, Rainbow.'

Clouds roll over the Harbour and there's lightning in the air. I've got the feeling that Pandora's nearby but I force myself to focus on the dame beside me. There's danger in that, too.

'Why did your parents call you Ariadne?'

'As a Renaissance couple my parents were interested in Greek legends.' It's too dark to see but I sense her shrug. 'According to mythology a king named Theseus was upset because a bunch of people called Cretans were sacrificing children to a bull-headed beast called the Minotaur. So Theseus offered himself as a sacrifice.'

'He must have wanted to die.'

Lightning flashes across the sky. In its glare the surface of the Harbour turns from printer's ink to shot silver while the shadow by the finger wharf stays black.

'No, he just wanted to put an end to the bloodshed.'

'He killed the Minotaur only to die anyway because he couldn't find his way out of the maze?'

'No, he escaped from the maze.'

'How did he do that?'

'A princess called Ariadne provided him with a clue.'

I know but I still ask. 'What do you mean?'

'The word *clue* doesn't mean what people think it means. *Clue* means *thread* and that's what Ariadne gave to Theseus – a ball of thread. *Unwind it as you go,* she told him, *and after you kill the Minotaur follow the clue.* That's how he escaped.'

'Then they lived happily ever after.'

'We need to find a shop, Rainbow.'

'What kind of shop?'

'A convenience store. We're about to rent a room in a sleazy, two-bit pub. To make up for it, at least we can have a real cup of coffee in the morning.'

Chapter 24

INTO THE MAZE

I shake my head.

'Mind if I call you Princess?'

Under the red, green and yellow of the shop's neons the dame smiles her *Giaconda* smile. 'You can call me anything except late to bed.'

'You're a fine memory and I'd like to keep it that way. I'm nothing but a gumshoe – a flash of lightning, a drum roll of thunder, too much darkness and too many clouds. Relationships don't go hand-in-hand with detecting – all we can ever be is friends.'

Ariadne shrugs; her mind's elsewhere. 'That's all very well, Rainbow, but I'm going shopping.'

A tall, bony dame in a frock that could have belonged to a pygmy is sprawled on a bench while a joker behind a cast-iron grille with a sign above it that used to read *NO SMOKING* but now reads *NO POKING* rolls ball-bearing eyes over Ariadne before asking the eternal question: *Hourly or weekly?*

I tell him all night, he names a price and I lean in to make sure he gets an eyeful of the gat. 'We're just renting a room,' I tell him, 'not buying the building.'

He replies that he spends his whole life dealing with smartarses which could account for the error. What he meant was that the aforementioned room's no longer available but he might be able to manage a smaller one at double the price. Ariadne shifts from one foot to the other like she's about to take over negotiations so I pay before he doubles again. He chucks me the same key he's been holding all the time.

We're assaulted by the smell of dust, too many years of bodily interaction and the ever-present promise of death. Too many stairs, followed by corridors piled high with dirty sheets and nowhere near enough illumination. I throw open the door to Room 231.

Welcome to Paradise.

The room's five paces long and six wide and reeks of industrial-strength disinfectant. There's a sideboard for making coffee without – as Ariadne predicted – anything to make it *with*, and a half-open package on the table next to the bed with a picture of a dame on it that might be a packet of after-dinner mints but isn't.

Ariadne places her purchases on the bench.

'You sure know how to spoil a girl.'

From the silence I deduce she's asleep. The storm's waned and the moonlight through the uncurtained window illuminates the sheen of her caramel skin, her tousled hair and a pair of wide-awake eyes staring back at me.

'I saw Irving Morris.'

'I trust he proved of assistance.'

'He didn't tell me anything I didn't know already.'

'He's chairman of his party's think tank, *The Way Ahead* committee, and has co-operated with Watchdog in our research into terrorism.'

'I need some information.'

'What about?'

'Going back to those *Troubles* …'

She shifts as far from me as she can without falling out of bed.

'Is this why you asked me out?' She lapses into silence and it's not the silence of the lambs. 'I thought you wanted me for myself – or at least for old times' sake.'

'Don't be like that, Princess.'

'I'm not being like *anything*. And stop calling me *Princess*.' She pauses; considers; decides. 'Very well, I'll tell you what you want to know.'

'It can wait until after.'

'Until after what?'

Until after what happens next. Which involves a lot of this and a little more of that which adds up to nothing in particular or something of everything, depending upon your point of view.

The next morning Ariadne is holding two mugs of fresh-brewed coffee out from her body so she's not in danger of burning herself. I notice the zig-zag marks on her stomach.

'You've had kids.'

She stops on her way to the bed. 'There was a child but it wasn't my husband's. I was in a relationship with someone else before we married. Actually my pregnancy was why James and I married. The father already had a wife so he wasn't available even if I wanted to marry him, which I didn't.' She changes the subject. 'What about you?'

'I got hitched, we had a kid and I lost both because I wasn't fit for husbandry.' My turn to change the subject. 'Ready to talk about the Troubles?'

She shrugs. 'It was industrial sabotage – with a twist.' She reaches the bed, stops, hands me the two coffees and climbs back under the covers, after which I hand her back her coffee. All of which takes time but I need time, in order to work out where this is going.

'What's the twist?'

'I told you – *terrorism.*'

Chapter 25

THE HOLES IN THE WALL

What's with the convergence of unrelated phenomena? Harry wanted to know. To which I replied: *While one thing doesn't necessarily follow from another, in the end it probably does. Which doesn't mean things that seem totally unrelated aren't.*

'What's *terrorism* got to do with anything?'

Ariadne takes a sip of her coffee.

'The popular view is men in masks doing beheadings, suicide bombers at embassies, hijackers, the Munich Olympics and people flying planes into tall buildings. But it's not as simple as that. You don't build businesses the size of ours without being different and James was – different. Before becoming a businessman, he was an officer in Vietnam in charge of supplying arms and ammunition. He diverted weaponry to people in the Middle East. He supplied well and they paid well.'

'Did you know this when you married him?'

Ariadne shakes her head so hard her coffee spills.

'Only afterwards when it was too late.'

'So things went bad after that?'

'On the contrary, things went extremely well. I

learnt to live with it and by the time the war was over, James was filthy rich. He bought goldmines and other lucrative enterprises and put the rest of his money into industry. As part of the money-making process, he financed politicians who helped him to become even richer. By then, politics had discovered a natural bedfellow – terrorism. Which meant that James had to tidy up his past or – despite his donations – politicians would cease to be his new best friends.'

'In other words he needed to cut the thread that linked him to his mates in the Middle East?'

'He was in deep. He made a lot of money and they expected a lot back. When he tried to break from them, they reacted badly. These extremists – they can't be called religious fanatics because they're not religious at all: they only use religion as an excuse for killing – declared a jihad on him. He became a marked man. That was when he set up Watchdog, to keep up to date with developments in terrorism. He passed on Watchdog's findings to the politicians. After his death, Watchdog continued.'

'Do the terrorists still bother you – now that he's dead?'

Ariadne nods. 'Don't they bother everyone? In our case they did things like cut brake lines and laid bombs. They shot the manager of one of our mines but we couldn't do anything in retaliation, even if we'd dared.'

'How did James die?'

'They shot him.'

'How come no-one heard about it?'

She takes a deep breath. 'The object of terrorism

is to terrify people and there wasn't an election at the time so it was hushed up. If jihadists could kill a rich and powerful man they could do anything. Terrorism thrives on terror and the government didn't want people terrified. Not just then, anyway –'

The small, black hole in the wall between our room and the room next door seem to appear *after* Ariadne's mug shatters. I roll her onto the floor and grab my gat from under the pillow. The hole looks like one made by a 0.40 which most likely makes the weapon a Para-Ordnance Tac-Forty.

'Stay where you are, Princess,' I tell her. 'They're listening for movement and if they hear any we're done for.'

I get out the door quiet and take the stairs three at a time to make as much height as possible as fast as I can. On the way, I loose off a volley that splinters the door of the adjoining room and brings an immediate shot in return.

The rest of the doors – I count eight – stay shut and all is silence because the punters have paid for an easy roll rather than a hard death. If Ariadne does what I told her she'll stay where she is. But she's not used to being told to do anything which means there are no guarantees. I get myself to the next floor, hotfoot it to the service stairs and start down again.

He's small and he's armed and when I burst through

the paper-thin wall into Room 233 he spins around gun-first. But he isn't expecting a house call from a wall, making him a split-infinitive too slow. I've got time to do a swan dive, which I'm about to follow up with a knee to the groin when –

I thought he had more than one gun or was a quick reloader but there was a third option and that was a second gunman. He's on the other side of the little man and his Tic-Tac-Toe's aimed at my ear. I've just got time to yell in the direction of the far wall, *'Run for it, Princess!'* before the slug gets me in the only part of my anatomy he can hit because the first gunman's in the way.

'Don't move!' screams Number Two.

I wipe the blood off my ear. There's a style about these two I haven't seen before. Or if I have, it's buried deep in memory – a coolness under fire that doesn't go with street thugs. The guns are high quality and matching – a combined 15.2 inches of death. But if you obey killers you're a dead man so instead of doing what I'm told I grab the first gunman, swing him over my head like I'm a principal *danseur* and he's a *danseuse* and chuck him at the second gunman just as he unleashes the follow-up.

Half a dozen slugs at close range are always going to find their mark even if the mark isn't their first choice and the little man's body jiggery-pokes like a puppet with its strings cut. He hits the floor as I dive for where I last saw the second gunman. But he's already out the door and I hear his feet clatter down the stairs as I turn to what's left of his mate.

He's lying face down, no more than a bale of

hay, a dead dog, a colander with six 0.40 holes in it – which is six too many if you want to live. I roll him over and go through his pockets to find that his clothes – apart from the flick knife in the shin sheath and the mobile phone in the silver case, both of which I take – are even emptier than his body.

Chapter 26

GOODBYE SWEETHEART

I get back to our room to find Ariadne already dressed.

'It's not enough to bring me to a brothel!' she shouts, shaking her head while gripping the doorknob with a hand even whiter than her face. 'Someone has to shoot my coffee out of my hand and –'

She's interrupted by what at first sound like violins but turn out to be sirens. I shrug on my clothes.

'If you try to leave by the front door the cops will arrest you on suspicion of whatever comes to mind. Also at the front door will be photographers which means that in the morning you'll find yourself staring from the front page of the tabloids and it won't be in company with a story about your community spirit. You'll go down in your shareholders' estimation and your company's shares will go down with it. The front door isn't an option.'

People don't like losing money, particularly when they can afford to. Ariadne hesitates. She who hesitates is raspberries. I grab her by her uncertainty and head for the fire escape.

That's how it goes in this game – from sin to rivalry to love and affection then back again in one easy lesson. In this case via the rear window of a brothel above a strip joint in a lowlife part of town clutching the hand of a memory with the cops after you. In places like this the law stops at the front door – like there's gold-plated armour between a brothel and the rest of the world. The Tax boys never visit, safety regulations go out the window along with people's morals and anyone can kill anyone else as long as they dispose of the body. We're two floors up and the fire escape's so rusty it wouldn't hold a rat.

'Was it a trick, what you said about share values?' Ariadne asks.

'Want to find out?'

'I'd rather not.'

'Then it's like I said, Princess – you're a slave to wealth and we got to go back inside.'

Back into the stinking corridors that are the dwelling places of sad secrets. *When you need to hide, make for where they least expect you.* I drag Ariadne through the warren of corridors and finally out a fire door at the rear of the building. I offer to accompany her back to her office but she declines.

It's between the hatch and the jamb on the deck door, a white envelope with nothing on the outside apart from the words: *CARE OF RORY*. I don't open it until I restart the pump, untangle the mooring rope, straighten my emotions, uncap the high-shouldered bottle of Glenlivet Number 18 and take a long swig as well as a deep breath. Only then do I thumb open the envelope.

Dear Daddy, I'm trying to put into practice what you taught me but it's not easy. Our teachers are rigorous about ethics, the same as you were. Along the driveway to the Police Academy stands a row of plastic posts with the words Excellence, Trust, Honour, Impartiality, Commitment, Accountability and Leadership on them. As you will have worked out, the initials spell ETHICAL. You'll be pleased to know I excel in shooting and thanks to you I'm not doing badly in other areas as well. But I'm not writing to brag — it's about a certain line I can't cross. They say any cadet crossing it will be thrown out.

So I can't help thinking what they'd say if they knew you were my father (in my application I wrote what's written on my birth certificate: Father Unknown*). I know you'll understand, Daddy, and also that I'll always love you. But if I'm to succeed here I need to break with you. I'm not a little girl any more. Which means I have to make my own way and that way must be without impediment. You're tough and you've dealt with a lot of people a lot tougher than I am so you'll cope. I'm seeing another cadet and he helps me make the hard decisions, of which this is one. You always wanted me to play it straight. What I'm saying is that we can't be in contact. Please respect my decision and don't try to call. Imogene.*

Impediment. Even in code, the word jumps out at

me. The kid –

But I can no longer call her that because – like she's been at great pains to tell me – she's no longer a kid, she's a *woman*. And the woman that used to be my daughter knows what an *impediment* is because I taught her: it's from the Latin *impedimenta*, meaning *unwanted baggage – something that gets in the way, a load too great to bear, a hindrance, an obstruction*, in other words … The day's stolen from me and all I'm left with is a blood-red sunset, a sinking boat and a set of unmatched fingerprints, courtesy of the gunman's phone and knife.

A death rattle wakes me and I drag myself out on deck to find the pump's stopped, it's late afternoon, Queen hasn't done his rounds and one of the phones is ringing. I fumble it out, click on and the death rattle ceases.

'What do you know?' says a voice.

I don't recognise the voice so I don't reply. The Harbour mirrors my feelings – a grey sky over a leaden sea that goes all the way down to Hades. I'm not thinking too clear and the voice on the other end of the phone doesn't help with my thinking.

'You still there, Sailor Boy?'

Chapter 27

MEET ME AT THE MORGUE

'What do you want?'

'It's not what *I* want, it's what *you* want,' the voice replies. 'Your own life mightn't be worth much but what about your nearest and dearest?'

'I don't know anything.' I choose my words careful, the way a drunk focuses on walking a straight line after a bad night. 'I thought I did but I don't. And I'm no longer investigating those deaths because nothing can bring those people back to life.'

'In other words you'll let sleeping dogs lie – a stupid policy, if I may say so, which could result in more innocent people dying. Anyway I don't believe you.' Pause. 'This will be death number – I've lost count – let's call it death number three. Look to windward.'

The voice clicks off and I'm left staring at a dead phone in a silver case which I recognise as the one belonging to the gunman in the brothel, which explains how they got onto me. I drop it like it's come out of a crematorium before doing like the voice said because I was never going to do anything else, and look to windward.

Grey cumulus clouds are sweeping in through the Heads. And aimed straight for the *Wooden No* is a familiar boat – a fishing smack of shiplap construction with a fisherman's gantry sticking up fore of the superstructure, a prow like a Roman nose and cadmium-yellow marks on the hull. A boat that – if it keeps on its course – will ram the *Wooden No*, sending it finally and forever to the bottom of the Harbour.

'Hey, Queen!' I yell.

Putt-putt-putt. The motor's throttled back to *Dead Slow* and it looks like a dead man's boat, empty of life, a ghost ship. It's no more than five fathoms distant and closing fast. I get myself to the railing, keeping an eye on the *Flying Dutchman* as I scrabble for the boat hook. Only it's not there because it's where I left it after untangling the mooring in a drunken stupor last night. Two fathoms. Ten feet. Eight. Five.

I heave myself over the side, brace myself against the rail, grab the Roman-nosed prow and lock my arms around it like a lover. Setting my shoulder against the hull I heave, feel Queen's craft start to turn, reluctantly letting itself be diverted. The *Wooden No* shudders as the smack hits her. I force my legs straight, feeling the veins in my temples bulge as timber shrieks against timber, using my ebbing strength to straighten, before pirouetting onto the smack as she slides by, at the same time scrabbling for the tiller. To find a length of wire twisted around it while the throttle's held in position with gum. I untangle the wire, strip off the gunk, haul at the tiller and cut the engine. The unmistakable smell of eau-de-cologne fights the stench of diesel but that's Queen, who's curled in the foetal position next to a couple of lobster pots, looking like the overgrown schoolboy he is.

Correction – *was*. Because Queen is no more. I find an anorak covered with fish scales, tuck it over his body and turn away. The tragic Harbour's just turned more tragic. Rube's gone, then Harry, now Queen. I climb back on the *Wooden No* just as the phone rings. I check the little window as I switch on. It's the same number.

'I'll do whatever you want,' I answer before the voice has a chance to put the question; I think of Imogene, Rory, Ariadne – people close to me who are still alive. 'Just stop the killings.'

But all the voice says is, 'In forty-five minutes, you're to meet me at the morgue.'

Rain's churning the Harbour to sandpaper as I hammer the coracle shoreward. I'm halfway there when I ring Roarer.

'Yeah?'

'You're still alive.'

'Thanks for letting me know.'

'This ain't a joke, Roarer, or I wouldn't be on an open line. Has anyone asked for a meet?'

'As it happens, yeah, someone called about a job.'

'A contract?'

'What other kind of job is there?'

'Anyone we know?'

'Only another low-life that had it coming.'

'I'm talking about the *client* not the corpse – is the *client* someone we know?'

'No, just someone with a rough voice, plenty of money and a grudge.'

'When and where's the meet?'

'At Victoria Park in half an hour.'

I'm due at the morgue just after that.

'What's the deal with the rock spider?'

'What rock spider?'

'The one that looks like you.'

'You mean Hertz?'

Diego Hertz, a creep that's hurt more innocent children than anyone wants to know; who's avoided jail only by dint of good lawyers and bad judges; someone even the *Terrorgraph* hasn't been able to get.

'Roarer?'

He comes halfway out of his stupor. 'You know what I think about Diego, Rain – people like that should be –'

'How quick can you contact him?'

'I know someone who knows someone who knows his number. So, yeah, pretty well straight away.'

'And how quick after that can you get him where we want him?'

'Depends where we want him.'

'At the swimming pool at Victoria Park.'

'Give me an hour.'

I give him an hour.

Chapter 28

THE WRONG DEATH

After I've dealt with Roarer I phone and ask the Voice for extra time and he seems happy to oblige, almost too happy, the rough tones going into overdrive and coming out even rougher.

'You just made a telephone call. Who to?'

'Santa Claus.'

'Laugh while you can, Rainbow. How long do you want?'

'Two hours.'

'I'll give you one.'

'I need two,' I reply. 'I got to get to shore, walk to Cammeray, wait for a bus, change at Town Hall and after that – well, you know what public transport's like.'

'One hour.'

'Two,' I repeat grimly.

'Ninety minutes tops.'

I note the flash of high-powered lenses as I row. The watcher's on a vessel not of these waters, a small cadmium-yellow speedster that – because of the paint marks on the hull of the fishing smack – has to be the craft they used for the Queen job.

The watcher's watching to make sure I follow instructions. I pretend not to notice. But who do I think I'm fooling?

The rain's stopped and the sign at the entrance to Victoria Park says skateboards, bikes and dogs are unlawful but there's nothing about murder. Me and Roarer watch events unfold – a couple of innocent picnickers minding their own business under a Moreton Bay fig.

'Any problems?'

Rory shrugs. 'My contact gave me the number of a screw who sold me Hertz's details and when I spoke to Hertz I pretended to be that other paederast – Mollie something or other. I told him I knew a kid who liked one-legged men.' Rory pulls a face – just talking to Hertz had to have hurt. 'I told him to dress like me and the bastard could hardly answer for excitement.'

The sun comes out and its light nestles among the indigo-coloured kale in the garden beds. The wet trees glisten like fresh blood while kids scream happily behind the chain-wire fence around the swimming pool. The bench by the path outside the fence is vacant. Rory gets a thought; it's rare but it happens.

'You're sending this guy to his death, Rain. I know he's bad but I got to ask: have you lost your moral compass?'

I shrug. 'Life's complex, Roarer, and death even

more so. It was either you or Hertz. And every day he's dead means another kid escapes his clutches.'

'Since when did you become Mr Retribution?'

'It's not about killing Diego. It's life that matters, not death. They were going to kill you – we're giving them someone else in your place who happens to be a bastard.'

'Why don't we just kill the killer?'

'Because we're dealing with a Hydra-headed monster, Roarer. Chop off one head and we'll end up with a whole lot more. We're up against a force we've never fought before. We got to kill the beast and make sure it *stays* dead. I'm hoping your *apparent* death will lead us to them.' I can see by the faraway look in Rory's eyes he doesn't understand and never will; I try again. 'These are the people who killed Rube and Harry and almost certainly will try to kill many more.'

I haven't told him about the latest murder so I tell him now.

'Queen's dead. I told the Water Cops which means Queen will be at the morgue and news of this latest apparently motiveless killing will be all over the media. We're deep in the labyrinth and if we lose the thread we might be lost forever.'

Just like Rory's lost the thread – but that happened long ago. I get in before he does.

'It's a case of better thread than dead, Roarer.'

The shadow's at ten o'clock high, up by the cutting edge of the university – an etiolated, bleak figure at odds with its environment, accompanied by the quickest of movements and the flash of a knife. But I can't let Pandora distract me. I look back to the pool. He's sitting on the bench reading a newspaper.

He's someone I've never seen before, tall but sufficiently well-trained to know he's got to compensate for his height in order to appear innocuous, a phone wire doubling as a hearing aid sticking out of his left ear as he sprawls on the park bench, his weight on his coccyx and his long legs stretched before him, conversing with his hearing aid while he pretends to be reading his newspaper.

I'm close enough to read the front page heading:

ANOTHER DEATH

Terrorism Tightens Noose

I'm also close enough to see the figure in the grey tracksuit – one pants leg pinned up – swinging across the park on crutches. And seeing him, I do a double-take, the sort of take you do when you see someone's double – in this case, Rory's.

I can just make out that the figure on the bench behind the newspaper is cuddling a Heckler & Koch USP – the Universal Self Loader – a pistol with pretty fair accuracy coupled with an extended barrel designed to take a suppressor. To a background of happy cries of unmolested children splashing in the sunlight and the stentorian shouts of teachers trying to shush them, the man on the bench shifts slightly and immediately afterwards a puff of incandescent smoke appears above the newspaper. The one-legged man's crutches spill silently onto the grass and the paederast follows.

It's five minutes before the arrival of the ambulance – during which time the teachers must have been informed of the killing and the kids herded out of the pool into their respective change rooms for the usual post-assassination counselling. The cops drive over the wet grass and the even wetter garden beds because they don't respect anything, not even death. It's only when they've got their crime-scene tape in place and the death van drives off with the body of the dead paederast, that I realise my error.

'They weren't cops, Roarer.'

'What do you mean? They were wearing uniforms, weren't they? And they were driving cop cars. Plus they were doing what cops always do after a crime.'

'That's just it, Roarer, they *didn't* do what cops do after a crime. For a start they were too quick and ditto the ambulance. Where's Forensics? And what happened to the police photographer? Cops don't take bodies to the morgue immediately after they become bodies – anything but. They leave things as they are and they look for clues and ask witnesses questions like: *Did you see anything unusual?* Someone's doing the cops' dirty work for them in order to keep the real cops out of the way.'

'But they *are* looking for clues.'

I look to where Rory's looking. There are five of them and they've got their Glocks out and they're prowling along the pool fence, poking at bushes and treading all over the garden beds.

I shake my head.

'They're not looking for clues, Roarer – they're looking for me.'

Chapter 29

THE FAVOUR OF THE MONTH

Terrorism Tightens Noose, the heading read. They were smart enough to kill Ruby, Harry and Queen and after that, via me, locate Roarer. They were also clever enough to see through my ruse. Which doesn't happen unless someone's a past master at second-guessing – a past master at staying in business as well as alive. They knew it wasn't Rory but went ahead anyway because another death – any death – would still serve their purpose.

'It's time to go, Roarer.'

'Why don't we just pot them?'

'Because potting people isn't the answer to everything – right now it's not even the answer to anything.'

Students are pouring out of the university in preparation for becoming an integral part of the workforce. As me and Roarer work our way into the crush the students come into sharp relief. Thin faces, young faces, a worried face, a happy one – tall, short, fat, skinny, male and female. Which reminds me that the world isn't some amorphous crowd but a collection of individuals. It matters. The lights change and we stay with the crowd as it makes its way along Glebe Point Road, keeping our heads down.

'Look, I get what you said about the pedo copping it instead of me,' Roarer says, swinging himself along on his crutch-gun as the students chatter around us. 'What I don't get is why I'd be a target in the first place.'

'Because you were associated with me in the first place.'

'So why doesn't whoever it is get rid of the middle man and just pot you?'

'Because these jokers …' Something's bothering me; I bother Rory with it. 'Look, I got a question, Roarer – did anyone get in touch with you after we spoke?'

'No.'

'Was there any way someone might have *overheard* you talking to Hertz?'

'Only the bloke outside the phone booth.'

'What bloke? Which phone booth?'

'The guy mending the road and the phone booth outside my place, the one that –'

'You got to go into hiding, Roarer.'

'Before or after we go to the morgue?'

I tell him we're no longer going to the morgue.

WILL WE EVER BE SAFE?

I flex my trapezia under the gabardine coat and bury my head behind the headline in the giveaway newspaper as the train clatters out of Central. The reason I wear bright clothes is because I disappear into obscurity when I'm not wearing them and I'm not wearing them now. I've put Rory into hiding as much as you can hide a one-legged assassin with half a brain but the old mortuary station just outside Central is a reminder – if one's needed – of what might happen if I become complacent.

I didn't identify myself but Imogene must have guessed who it was because she wouldn't come to the phone. Going to see her was my second option but I change my mind when confronted by the headline. There's a pattern here and I don't like patterns. I get out at Redfern, find a public telephone that works and call Ariadne.

'Ms Sidonia isn't in.'

'Tell her it's a matter of life or death.'

'She's still not in.'

I break every rule in the book. 'Tell her it's Rainbow.'

Once we were kids but now I'm a two-bit detective and she runs an empire. I had my chance and I blew it. It's not just a desk between us – I'm trying to bridge an abyss.

'I thought we weren't going to see each other again,' Ariadne says stiffly.

'That was then and this is now. Something's happened.'

'Apart from my getting shot at in a brothel?'

'My daughter's in danger and I need your help.'

'I've already helped by putting you in touch with Irving Morris. But Irving said you didn't seem interested.'

'Irving Morris was more concerned with pushing his own barrow than helping me with mine.'

'You wanted an *in* to the Troubles and he was it.'

I change the subject. 'Remember when I saved you from Parkinson?'

Ariadne looks uncomfortable. 'We were kids. It was a long time ago.'

'It was near the bubblers. He had you in a headlock and you were crying. I managed to get you away and paid for it afterwards.'

'What you're saying is that it's my turn to help.'

'It's just something I remembered, Princess.'

Chapter 30

THE RED HERRING

'What do you want?'

A weak man kills, an honest one lies and the pacifist goes to war – you don't play tiddly-winks with fortune when your kid's life's at stake. After I tell her what I want, Ariadne reaches for the red phone nestled between the green and yellow ones and dials.

'This is Ariadne Sidonia. Is that Minister Caxton and is this line secure?'

'You have my word.'

'I don't want your word, Caxton, I want a secure line.'

'I'm sorry, yes, the line's secure.'

'Okay, listen. I'm calling in a favour – one of many, incidentally, that your party owes me.'

'It's real nice to hear from you, Ariadne. How can I –?'

'It's Ms Sidonia.'

'I'm sorry, Ms Sidonia. How can I help?'

'I need you to send a police officer to Mars.'

'State or Federal?'

'State.'

She glances at me. I nod confirmation. The politician chuckles ingratiatingly.

'Been speeding again, Ms Sidonia?'

'None of your business. Just do it.'

'But it's a State matter and I'm a Federal minister, remember.'

'And *you* remember that I'm Ariadne Sidonia.'

'I'm sorry. What are the specifics?'

'I need a police cadet sent to the Outer Hebrides.'

'Name?'

I tell Ariadne and Ariadne tells the Minister. 'And Caxton?' she adds.

'Yes, Ms Sidonia?'

'You're to call the NSW Police Minister *now*, he's to contact the chief of the police academy *now*, the transfer to the secret location is to be immediate and if anything goes wrong you're out on your neck, got me?'

It's Baisson Primary coming out in her.

'Very well, Ms Sidonia. In return, I have some news for you.'

He's a dog begging. Ariadne switches off *Speaker* and while she's listening her face goes white and when she hangs up it's translucent.

'It's going to happen.'

'What's going to happen?'

'What I feared. Something terrible.'

'Can you give me a clue?'

'That's just it – there *are* no clues. ASIO are checking it out but Caxton wants to know what Watchdog can discover.'

'Is there a *when, where, what* or *how*?'

Ariadne shakes her head. 'Just *when* – tomorrow, Australia Day.' A thought strikes her. 'Why – what are you going to do?'

I tell her something other than what I'm going to do.

The *Wooden No*'s where I left her but that doesn't mean she's safe. I stop rowing, tap into the onboard Secur-A-Cam from the safety of the skiff and scroll through the day's imagery. No sign of untoward activity: the pictures are grey-filtered nothingness – scenes of an innocent Harbour tilting this way and that as the boat sways; of moored vessels ducking and weaving; of ferries passing; scullers sculling; dads taking their kids for a sail.

There's been no visitors apart from gulls and cormorants but that doesn't mean there won't be. I climb aboard, restart the pump, find the paper with Babychino's address on it plus the first-aid kit, load Rube's box of tricks into the coracle, do a final check, get the oars back into their manacles and set about putting as much distance as possible between me and the *Wooden No*. She doesn't explode.

'Who's speaking?'

It's tomorrow and the voice is distant but my life's made up of distant voices. Also I'm no stranger to the clicks saying someone's listening in on the conversation.

'I can't say.'

'Oh, it's you.' Silence for a moment. 'What do you want?'

'The use of your second residence – the caravan in the forest off the Workhorse Parkway.'

'I like your hide asking.'

'I like my hide, too – which is why I'm asking.'

One day intimacy, hatred the next. I don't ask Tsunami what she's done since our last meeting – the less said the better because I don't want whoever's listening to suspect I'm deliberately feeding them information.

Tsunami fills the silence. 'Make sure you leave the van clean.'

'That goes without saying.'

But all I'm talking to is echoes and a series of clicks. I call Roarer on the same open line. Which means the same closed party will be listening.

'I need to go to a caravan in the forest off the Workhorse Parkway. I'll be outside the burger palace at the Cross in ten. Repeat our arrangement back to me.'

Rory does what he's told and whoever's bugging us can't fail to make the connection.

Chapter 31

THE MANEATER

Rory's in one of those American cars without a back that was here one day, gone the next – cream-ducoed with tiny windows behind the rear seat and a sidestep walkway – a 1940-something de Soto. I chuck Rube's box inside, climb in next to Roarer and glance in the rear-vision mirror. They're in a Hummer, black, with tinted windows. High vehicles, Hummers.

I turn to Rory. He's a mess. 'Pull yourself together, Roarer.'

'That's easy for you to say but I been trying to tidy up my private life. Janet won't leave the Fat Man, I'm in debt up to my bald patch and I'm having difficulty breaking back into the death game because I'm no longer in the Yellow Pages. Apart from which, word-of-mouth's telling would-be clients I've retired.'

'Where's the hearse?'

'I sold it. Where are we going?'

'*Not* to the caravan in the forest. I want you to head in that direction, lose the tail and end up *not* going to the caravan.'

'And after that?'

I don't want to overload him – his brain must be close to bursting.

'I'll tell you after you lose them.'

I'll say this much for Roarer, he can drive. One-legged or not, half-brained or with no brain at all, he's got the tail acting like the ball attached to the racquet I gave Imogene for her eighth birthday – or was it her tenth? Where we go, the Hummer follows. We turn right, the Hummer turns right; we exit City Street, so does the Hummer; we slip up a side road, the Hummer slips straight up after us.

'I'd prefer you not let them know that we know they're following us, Roarer.'

'How do I do that?'

'You can stop all these Dixie little manoeuvres for a start.'

There'll be at least three thugs in the Hummer and three into two won't go. We could waylay them but we need to stay alive. I peer through my half of the de Soto's split windscreen.

'What are you looking for?'

'A supermarket.'

'Are we going shopping?'

'Ever wonder why you never see Hummers in supermarket car parks? It's because they're too big. That thing behind us happens to be a 2006 model complete with balloon tyres which put it well over the two-metre mark. Know those signs in supermarket car parks that say *HEIGHT 2 METRES*? Well, what we're looking for is a sign that says –'

'I'm not stupid, Rainbow.'

It's getting on for lunchtime, the newspapers say we're headed for the greatest Australia Day ever and Babychino's still small, still oversexed and still having trouble with her tear ducts.

'This might sound silly,' she sighs, mopping at her beautiful eyes with a handkerchief big enough to sleep in, 'but every time someone knocks, I think it's Harry.'

The joint's a doll's house – a two-up, two-down, dunny-out-the-back terrace in North Sydney. I swing to cover the figure by the back door, gat uncocked and a slug already on the launch pad, only to find it's only a department store dummy dressed like Harry. A photo of the lovers making cats' eyes at each other is sitting on a record machine. I garage the gat.

'It looks like you miss him.'

'It's not just looks.' Babychino slumps on a sofa. 'Harry treated me like a queen and you ask if I miss him!'

'Did he leave you anything?'

'Apart from the memories?'

'Apart from the memories.'

'Yes, this house.'

'Anything else?'

'A life insurance policy worth a million.'

'A *million*?'

She nods, unaware of the irony in the eyebrow raise – or if she isn't unaware, doesn't show it. 'As you probably know, Harry was a successful bookie before he got into the hospitality industry. Yes, he could look after me and he did. He also made me laugh – eleven times out of ten his jokes were at his own expense.'

'Have you had any trouble since his death? Thugs heavying you, anonymous phone calls, men with shaven heads standing over you in buses?'

Babychino shakes her head. 'Harry was careful. He kept me hidden like a genie in a bottle – he didn't even tell you about me because he said you attracted criminals like flies to a sheep's bum.'

It doesn't sound like Harry. Also I could think of better ways of putting it.

'Do you know who killed him?'

'I never saw his killers.'

'Was he scared of anyone?'

'Harry was scared of his own shadow.'

Time to put the real question. 'Were you involved in his death?'

She doesn't even pause for breath. 'Harry made me laugh.'

Which is why she's crying now. I change the subject. 'I need somewhere to stay.'

'You can stay here – I owe that much to Harry.'

When the phone rings, the dame answers and afterwards she shows me to a bedroom the size of a broom cupboard.

'I don't want to profit from others' misfortune,' she

says, naming a figure even more generous than her own. 'I need a deposit for the key but you can come and go as you please.'

I hand over enough moolah to rent the main hall of the Sydney Opera House, park Rube's box and see Roarer off the premises.

'You okay?' he asks.

'Why shouldn't I be?'

He glances behind me. 'Because she's a man-eater and you're a man.'

Chapter 32

PATIENCE AND SHUFFLE THE CARDS

It's not hard to get information when people owe you favours. Wills are wills and someone's got Harry's. The ring-around takes ten minutes by the end of which I've learnt what I already suspected – Harry left nobody nothing. I set the index cards aside and open Rube's diary to the first entry. Music floats up the stairwell – Babychino's playing Doris Day playing at singing. Rube was tough but her diary reminds me she was also human.

There's a quote from Cervantes: *Paciencia y barajah.* Rube taught me enough Spanish for me to know this means: *Patience and shuffle the cards.* So I do like the quote says and work out the cards are pointers to Rube's cases, in alphabetical order and cross-referenced. *Allbricht, Arthur; cross-references: Murder; Corruption, Police; Horder, Lillian … Amhurst (company name); cross-reference: Drugs; Murder; Corruption, Police … Aperville (location of Hooligan HQ),* cross-references: *Conrad, James; [a list of names]; Drugs; Murder; Corruption, Police; Terrorism …* One of Rube's sayings was: *Never discount connections.* Which is why I don't discount what must be close to the last word she ever uttered – *indigo* or *indiquo* or … I go back to the Cervantes quote. *Paciencia y barajah – Patience and shuffle the cards.* What's *indigo* in Spanish? Or what sounds like *indigo* in Spanish? Another song starts and I picture Babychino teeny-bopping to the music as she tries to cope with the memory of Harry.

Rube's diary again: *Don't discount connections.* But the evidence is only *circumstantial.* Which in Spanish is: *indicios vehementes* which gives me *indicio* which looks more like *indigo* than it sounds, but Roarer was the filter. The music switches to ABBA while I try to make the connection. *Indicio* means *clue.* And what, long ago, did someone say about *clue*? Without warning the music stops.

It doesn't just stop – it comes to a screaming halt in the middle of the song that brought ABBA to prominence, followed by a crash, a scream, then silence.

The cards scatter as I head for the stairs. I came here for refuge but that's not what I'm getting. The stairs turn into a slippy-slide as the front door slams and a motor starts. Not one motor – two. The word's stuck in my head: *indicio.* What's it mean? *Thread,* that's right, it means *thread.* Where's Babychino, the dame who said she had a million good reasons to mourn Harry's passing, but hasn't? Going by the mess downstairs, she's gone straight into the loving arms of a death worse than fate.

I get myself into the street, find nothing and return via the back door – always return via the back door – to find two of them, young, fit, of medium height, one pale, the other swarthy. I'm not expecting them but they're expecting me even less. Swarthy's on the ground floor clutching Rube's box while Whitey's coming down the stairs with a high-velocity Tac-Five automatic in his belt, staring at the broken-down front door where I'm supposed to be.

It's an impossible shot, one-o'clock high through the banisters with the gramophone blocking my sightlines, so I leave my gat where it is and opt for the dive, bringing my knees up to my chest, grabbing my shins, curling my head into my sternum and hurling myself over the gramercy, uncoiling myself just as Whitey reaches the last step but one.

The trouble with weapons is that when people are carrying they forget their natural armoury – hands, elbows, knees, shoulders, feet. Instead they think they got to go for the gun. And while Whitey's going for his gun, I grab his foot, twist and lift and he goes over the side like a bleached tomato. *Keep him alive,* I tell myself. *Live men tell tales and I need tales.* I reach for Swarthy but he steps up and back, at the same time hurling Rube's box. It catches me in the chest, knocking me towards the broken-down door.

Like the tag-team in the brothel, these jokers know their way around brawls. While Swarthy gets ready for the follow-through, his mate kicks the record player out of the way and brings up his gat. I got the light behind me. Whitey blinks as he tries to adapt his peepers. I feint and his eyes follow as I go into a *plié* like I'm about to fly but instead stay on the ground and do a *glissé*.

The Para-Ordnance has the capacity to inflict maximum lethality in minimum time. Which is what it does as Whitey unleashes all nineteen slugs where his half-blind eyes tell him I'm headed – into the air where his mate is. Caught by the volley, Swarthy drops at the designated acceleration of thirty-two feet per second per second. I hurtle over the body to where I last saw Whitey to find that he's gone, leaving nothing but the upturned record player plus the stench of cordite and eau-de-cologne. I set the machine upright and it picks up where it left off.

My *Telefunken* rings.

'Yeah?'

'It's Rory.'

'What do you want?'

'It's a good thing I stayed.'

'Stayed where?'

'At the dame's. You told me to go but I didn't. It was a good thing I didn't, wasn't it?'

'Why?'

'Because I was able to tail them. They went through the lights at Cammeray and –'

'Where's Babychino?'

'She was in the car with the remaining hood. They got tangled in traffic, the offside rear door opened, the dame jumped out, the traffic cleared and the hood had to clear with it.'

'And you followed the car rather than sticking with the dame?'

'A man with one leg's as good as the next man only if he's armed or he's driving.'

'Where are you now?'

Rory tells me where he is. There's nothing I can do for Swarthy. On the way out I pick up the photo of Babychino and Harry gazing into each other's eyes because they're so much in love. Maybe too much in love.

An hour north of Sydney, gum trees unfurl into a vista of water dotted with islands. TERRIGAL, I read on the station sign but somehow it comes out *Terror-gal*. It could be paradise but the outer-Sydney suburb of Bridgetown is more like a murder house – looks nice but no-one in their right mind wants to live there. There's only one cab and the driver's asleep. I wake him.

'What's the quickest way to the shops?'

He blinks up at me. 'Depends whether you're going by cab or walking.'

'I'm walking.'

'That's the slowest way.'

I let him have his little joke because all I wanted was for him to remember the man with the wooden box asking directions. I find a speedboat called *Loverbuoy* bobbing at the end of a wharf with a dinghy beside it, while the pair of lovers that belong to it gaze into each other's eyes in the Pierless Restaurant. I double back to the station.

They call them *cells*, Ariadne explained. *For greater efficiency, terrorists divide themselves into cells. At least they used to but our research says that they're changing tactics. More and more, they're acting in pairs or alone. We think it's due to the 'bikie laws' the government brought in, making it an offence to associate with known criminals. But it seems that was the way the terrorists wanted to play it anyway.*

Rube, Harry and Queen are dead and Rory was set to join them. At least they can't get at Imogene. There were two killers in the brothel and, after that, another pair visited Babychino. To all intents and porpoises, the actions were spontaneous – ad hoc, arranged for the purpose, special. *The anti-terrorism people describe it as their worst nightmare,* Ariadne went on. *When they operate as individuals or in pairs it means there are no mass text messages, emails or phone-outs; there's no planning to eavesdrop on because there's no planning – just the intent to kill, followed by the kill.*

Chapter 33

IN THE COUNTRY
OF THE BLIND ...

The de Soto's half-hidden by scrub a hundred paces from the cluster-pack of Mercedes, BMWs, Lexuses, Audis and the Hummer with the crunched roof, while Roarer's slumped so far down behind the wheel only the top of his head and the tip of his crutch are visible. The joker limping towards the de Soto is carrying a Giandoso TZ45 – a different weapon to the one he had in the caravan park but it's the same knee. A swarm of ants finds me.

The day the bullies at school smeared me with treacle and tied me to an ants' nest I was saved by the fact that the small ants behind the gym – unlike these bigger ones – were more interested in the treacle than in me. These ones are already under my trouser legs and rapidly moving north.

Option 1: Ignore the ants and take the gunman.

Option 2: Dislodge the ants.

There's no choice so I take it. I drop Rube's box and hurtle towards the de Soto, shouting as I run. The gunman calls on me to stop because he's seen too many movies, his warning's followed by a single shot and the shot's followed by silence.

Turns out Rory wasn't asleep.

He's a good shot, Roarer. Knows where it kills, where it wounds, where it's only going to hurt. The bullet's found its way through the tendons, bones and veins like a grub through a rotten apple. The limping joker with the Giandoso TZ45 will walk again, talk again and pick his nose again. I haul out the first-aid kit, tourniquet his arm, apply mercurochrome, bandage the hand, then do the wrists-and-ankles back-truss, gagging him in case he feels the urge to scream. Then I sling him in the boot of the de Soto along with Rube's box. The boot's got built-in air holes – if he dies, it won't be the fault of the manufacturers.

A set of worn sandstone steps leads to double doors, across the top of which a faded blue sign reads: *STRANGEFELLOWS' HALL, 1881* – printed at a time when the world still acknowledged apostrophes. The joint's white with a green corrugated roof and pointy windows, set high.

'What are *strangefellows*?' Rory asks.

'The name's ironic – they were pillows of the community.'

'What are they now?'

'Dead.'

'Why are we here?'

'Because Rube, Harry and Queen are also dead and at the Victoria Park swimming pool you nearly joined them.'

We let the air out of the tyres by depressing the valves instead of knifing the tubes because that would make too much noise and right now I happen to like my privacy. We don't do the Hummer because its oversized tyres are wearing valve locks and disabling the alarm would take more time than we got.

'What do we do now?'

'We shut up.'

'After we shut up.'

'We go round the back.'

As well as working alone and in pairs, terrorists still also use cells, Ariadne said. There are dozens throughout Sydney and each one's a stand-alone — which means the right hand doesn't know what the left hand's doing. They've redoubled their efforts since we followed America into its latest war and — like the Irish Republican Army and any other terrorist group you care to name — they have one aim and that is to cause as much terror as possible. As a safeguard, the cells work independently of one another.

I haul out the gat and motion Roarer to follow as I work my way along the side of the building. The windows are too high to see through, the path's cracked and a steel fence screens the hall from its neighbours. There are no spider webs, the electrical board's been read recently and the trip wire's close to invisible. I warn Roarer before high-stepping over it.

If anything's going on inside the hall I can't hear it. What did I expect? The sound of goose steps? Rifle fire? People cheering a beheading?

Behind the hall, the trees are carved, the lawn's mown and the smell of fresh-cut grass takes me back to Hopesville where I met the dame of my dreams, Salina, and convinced myself that my Aunt Rube was weird, my dead mum and hippie dad were aberrations and detective work was for the birds. The feeling lasted as long as it took to realise that the real aberrations were marriage and the lawn.

The roses covering the trellis are nicely tended and the table's clear of leaves. Beyond the fence with the panel missing the jungle takes over. But here, birds sing and the window throws back a double reflection, the kind that usually only comes with cheap mirrors.

The sun's at a bad angle but I haven't got time to wait for a good one. While Rory parks his crutch, I look at the reflections – of Roarer and, behind him, the well-tended lawn. After my eyes stop doing gymnastics, I make out that the figures on the other side of the double-glazing aren't doing gun drills or learning how to make bombs or being harangued by a demagogue in a kaftan. Instead, a couple of dozen suits are focused on a speaker.

He's small, smiling and somehow familiar. Dark hair, small head, tight mouth and even from here I can see the calculating expression in the bright little pinpoint eyes. Because of the double-glazing I can't hear what he's saying but there's more ways of killing a cat than covering it with yak fat and baking it. I read his lips.

'To quote the master,' he's saying: '*You should not deviate from what's good if that's possible but you should know how to do evil if necessary.*'

He pauses to show that he's finished quoting but also to make sure that he's got his audience's attention. He has. He's got mine, too.

'Remember: Increased terrorism means greater surveillance – more tapped phones, less secure internet communication, more cameras; the power to arrest and confine will increase exponentially; the government might arrogate to itself the right to expel an entire community. Are you ready for tonight?'

I don't need to lip-read to know that on these last words the room erupts – the vibrations are enough. The faces as they turn to their neighbours are radiant and the hall shakes with the stamping of feet. Young feet and young faces, with nice haircuts like the lawn, close-shaven cheeks pink with emotion. *The master?* Who's *the master?* Or did little Mephistopheles say *martyr?*

'Don't move!'

The scene in the reflective window shifts like an amoeba. We got company. 'Turn slow or don't turn at all,' the company says. 'The window's bulletproof as well as soundproof which means I can send any number of slugs your way and after they've gone through you they'll bounce harmlessly off your reflections. And you can take your hand away from that piece you're carrying under your jacket.'

I turn, slow. Sex: *male;* Age: *25–27;* Description: *medium height, stocky build, brown hair cut respectable, blue eyes;* Clothes: *cabbage-tree hat, baggy pants thong-tied below the knees, coated with dried grass-mush and held up with braces, collarless shirt. Conclusion: what I should have guessed but didn't — that a big, nice-tended garden means there's a tender. Or maybe not so tender. Add-on extra: machine-gun with silencer, held professional in the big hands, pointed at me but light in the nozzle meaning it's also aware of the existence of Roarer. Further information: confident smile — too confident.*

I could go for the gat but that wouldn't be clever. He's dappled in shadow but there's nothing attractive about the holograph because of the gun. It's what the Birmingham Small Arms people dubbed the *Essie* — short for *Silent Sten*, due to the integrated muffler — and its hollow stock's tucked into his waist, one big, gnarled hand's on the silencer and the other's around the trigger guard. The black hole at the end of the barrel's pointed at my chest. The Essies were discontinued because of the tendency of the silencer to melt under sustained fire but the gun still kills.

'I said *don't move.* That means you, one leg, as well as the oaf in the Akubra.'

'We're looking for Pete,' I tell him. 'But we must have the wrong address so we'll give our apologies and get out of your hair.'

The bullet takes out the toe of my left whiteside, the smell of gunpowder mingles with the scent of roses and the expression on the gardener's face doesn't change because there's no expression.

Chapter 34

... THE ONE-EYED
MAN IS DEAD

'Let's go for a little walk.' The gardener flicks his weapon at Rory. 'Pick up your crutch.' Rory does like he's told and the gunman flicks the Sten back at me. 'Now take the gun out of its holster and drop it. Slowly.'

I go to reach inside my coat but the gunman waves *No* at me with the Sten. 'The other hand.'

My Smith & Wesson clatters to the pavers; the gunman jerks his gun at Rory. 'You, too.'

'I don't carry.'

Rory lifts his crutch-gun and suddenly there's much more expression in the gunman's face than there has been up to now, a sort of inclination of the head that could be quizzical, what looks like a laugh in the region of the mouth and, in the middle of his forehead, a hole that looks like an eye.

'You haven't lost your touch, Roarer.'

Nothing goes according to plan, especially when there isn't one. Unlike the Sten, Roarer's gun doesn't possess a silencer and its blast could waken the dead. Boots clatter along the walkway which means that, as a means of egress, it's no longer an option. I head for the arbour.

'Shake a leg, Roarer!'

'It's all I got!'

The ants I had up my trousers are nothing compared with the mob pouring out of the hall, led by Mephistopheles. It's going to be touch and go – if they touch us, we're gone.

'Want me to mow 'em down, Rain?'

'They're not grass and we ain't gardeners, Roarer!'

Our pursuers are only thirty paces behind by the time we reach the car. I download the joker from the boot – he's still alive – and grab Rube's box as Roarer gets behind the wheel. I start across the road.

'Aren't you coming with me?'

They're almost on us but with Rory you got to explain everything. 'I got a previous engagement. You know what to do.'

He guns the motor; it sounds like a bunch of tin cans doing the Watusi; yeah, he knows what to do.

'I lead 'em a merry dance.'

'And if they catch you?'

'I shoot 'em.'

'Wrong answer – the right answer is you won't *let* them catch you. Now *go*!'

The speedboat's still at the far end of the pier, its dinghy bobbing by its side. I get myself into the restaurant, lean down and take Lothario by the arm.

'Sorry to interrupt your little tryst,' I tell him, 'but I'm taking you for a ride.'

He puts up a fight but I tell the waiter Lothario's my best friend and we always do it this way when he's drunk. I drop an extra fifty on top of the bill by way of compensation and a half-Nelson on my new best friend does the rest. The dame gets a fit of the giggles and she's still giggling as we board *Loverbuoy*.

'You've kidnapped us because you think we own this boat when we don't,' she gurgles. 'Which means you have to let us go. It also means that the *real* owners are going to realise what you've done and before you get halfway down the coast the cops will stop you.'

Like I said, nothing goes according to plan – even when there is one.

'I guess you're some kind of terrorist,' she goes on. 'Which makes you halfway exciting, which is more than Bombshell here is.'

I throw myself on the mercy of the Fates; there's nothing else to throw myself on.

'Got any ideas?'

'We could take my ute.'

She leads me to a battered Falcon, which she gets started and up the road to the highway. I tuck Rube's box between us, the wireless is playing *Deep Purple* and the dame's swaying to the music like she's at sea.

Babychino's got the door back on its hinges and the innocent look back on her face. 'Where did you go?' she squeaks.

I ignore the question because I've got a few of my own. 'How did you escape?'

'The car was held up by traffic and my abductor wasn't looking so I took off.'

'Do you expect me to believe that?'

'What do you think happened?' I don't tell her what I think happened; tell her what I think happened and I'll alert the Cookie Monster and I don't want to alert the Cookie Monster. She gives up on that question and asks another one. 'Are you staying?'

'What happened to the corpse?'

'What corpse?'

'The one full of bullets I left sprawled at the foot of the stairs.'

'I don't know what you're talking about.'

Chapter 35

OUT OF THE FRYING PAN ...

Tsunami's in. She's dressed in black and I sense rather than see the dame that's as high as a kite on ecstasy behind me peering across from her ute.

'I need you for a job.'

'What if I say no?'

'Like they say in the song, Tsunami: you're just a girl that can't say no, not when lives depend on it, not when your country's calling you.'

That gets me a half-smile. 'And what's my country saying?'

I tell her what her country's saying and after she says she's not having any more to do with me, I climb back in the ute where it's the drug dame's turn to ask questions. She's just started to ask them when Tsunami trots across to me. I wind down the window.

'All right, I'll do it,' she says.

'Why the change of heart?'

She shrugs. 'I've always had a heart and that's my problem. Like you said, life's not a bowl of cherries and you have to eat what's put in front of you. Well, you're in front of me and –' she peers in the car,

'– who's she?'

I do the introductions but it's like I never spoke. There's a lot of silence until we reach Cammeray, where we part company with the drug dame, I tuck Rube's box under my arm, and me and Tsunami go the rest of the way on foot.

We can't stay at Babychino's because I no longer trust her and we can't go to the *Wooden No* because they know about the boat and I don't want to compromise Rory by going to his place. There's only one position vacant and after we finagle our way through the front door, we find the lift out of order and have to take the stairs to the fourth floor. I pick the lock and we're embraced by the cold, dark flat that used to be Harry's.

Tsunami looks around like she's back in the Army in a house with a bomb in it. 'Why are we here?'

'We got to hole up somewhere for a couple of hours and this is it. You can catch up on your beauty sleep.'

We're in the middle of a blackout, shadows flickering on the walls like the place is suffering early-onset dementia. By the light of my torch, I rework my way through Rube's files, after which I return to the diary. Like someone once said, misfortune's not necessarily the beginning of the end, it can be the end of the beginning. Rube, Harry and Queen are dead and nothing will change that.

Why didn't Harry tell me about his squeeze?

Babychino said Harry told her it was because I attract trouble like flies to a sheep's bum but what's that got to do with March hares? We were mates. I haul out the picture. There they are, gazing into each other's eyes, proof-positive they were lovers.

It's an old photograph because Harry hasn't yet acquired the scar that happened about ten years ago. So they been together that long? She must have been no more than a babe in arms when they met. I stare at her baby face. Still the same damp eyes and pouting lips – in ten years she hasn't aged at all when she should have. I look back at Harry – no scar, which means the photo was taken *before* the window was broken, the window behind Babychino with the sticker in the corner.

Harry's stamp collection's still on the old sideboard and with it his Sherlock Holmes magnifying glass. I hold the magnifier over the sticker: *A GLASS ACT – all pane, no pain.* But how could Harry have a new window but not the old scar?

I examine the photograph more closely and that's when I see it – a carefully photoshopped join between the dame's new face and Harry's old one.

They were never together.

I hear the sound of the lift rumble into life. *How can a lift work in the middle of a blackout?* I wake Tsunami. It's a two-metre leap to the downpipe, the kind people made before they realised downpipes didn't need to last beyond the next generation. The lift stops and the doors open as we shin down.

If indigo's the colour of memory, it's also the colour of the darkness in the courtyard. Four floors above us, I make out the flicker of torches. They'll see the open window soon enough and know where we are. I give Tsunami a leg-up over the wall and get over after her, my whitesides sloshing in the ripe fruit of a mulberry tree. I move but I move slow, hampered by the weight of Rube's box, the mulberries and the implications of the photo of Harry and Babychino.

Ariadne's wearing the face of someone forced to drink hemlock.

'I'm a person of great importance to the Australian economy, Rainbow – it's unfair to ask me to risk my life on business that's properly the province of the police. You know the old saying: *When I became an adult I put away childish things.* Well, we're adults now, we're grown up, we're different.'

I shake my head. 'Childish things have a habit of bouncing back into contention, Princess. We're the same as we always were – we just wear bigger clothes and carry more burdens.' Her face is pale in the moonlight. 'You've tried every other angle – paying their ransom demands, bowing to blackmail. Even, I suspect – on the basis that if you can't beat 'em, join 'em – working alongside them, doing their bidding so that your business will prosper.'

Ariadne hasn't taken to Tsunami, who's got her own thoughts, and I'm still trying to work out Babychino. Why did she make out she was Harry's lover when she wasn't? Why the elaborate photo set-up? She couldn't have come up with that on her own, which means she's working for somebody she shouldn't be. The cab winds its way out of Ariadne's labyrinth and along New South Head Road, the Harbour on our right and the money on our left. It's not until we reach Rushcutters Bay that Ariadne speaks.

'Who's she?'

'She's a professional and we're going to need a professional.'

'Why do you need me, then?'

'I think you know the answer to that.'

The night looms and I hear the cackle of what sounds like Pandora's laughter. Nothing's changed and everything's different. Ariadne stares out the window. What she's seeing might be anything and the laughter no more than the sound of silence.

Chapter 36

... INTO THE FIRE

Because of the fireworks, Sydney Harbour's a no-go zone. The barriers are up and the cops and security people are marshalling the foot traffic – families out for a picnic, lovers, schoolkids, groups from old people's homes, drunks. There's to be two lots of fireworks, both on the Bridge – the first in an hour's time, the second at midnight.

Ariadne glances at Tsunami then back at me. 'We really should be calling the police, Rainbow. I know these people. Didn't you hear me tell the Minister to have your daughter moved to a safe house? I know the police commissioner and God knows who else. Just a word from me and –'

'And what?' We're out of the cab; I hustle her through the crowd and Tsunami follows. 'There had to be a time in your life when your power hits the wall and this is it, Princess. We're not playing Happy Families, this is for real. The world as we know it is set to end and somehow we got to see it doesn't.'

In daylight, people inhabit an oasis. The city stands four-square to the Harbour and the shadows of tall buildings are somehow comforting. People hurry to and from work and the traffic edges sedately around them. The light's a safety net.

But right now the city's a hellhole. The traffic's stopped at the edge of the Criminal Behaviour District – the CBD – and everything's reduced to shadows. The Bridge is hostage to darkness. Now and again a face looms out of the shadows but just as quickly looms in again while the voices around us wear padded shoes. If the crowds go where they're told they'll be lambs to the slaughter. It's a bad image and I try to dispel it but can't – we're beasts in a holding yard and the only way out is via the abattoir.

'We gotta talk, Princess.'

'We've already talked.'

'Then we gotta talk some more.'

Images shuffle through my head but they're not the right images. Because all mixed up with them are suicide bombers, Guy Fawkes preparing to blow up London's Houses of Parliament and planes flying into tall buildings in New York. Why us, why innocent Sydney – innocent, at least, of offending on the international stage? *Because we declared war on Islamic State*, Ariadne explains. *We're the mouse that roared and it appears that someone was listening.* Tsunami's silent.

'Let's go through it all again, Princess, only slower this time. You're hand in glove with the politicians, right?'

'It depends what you mean by *hand in glove* ...'

'This is no time to be coy. Something's about to happen and you're the only one with anything that might be called a clue to what it will be. Let me get this straight: there's your Watchdog department and then there are the politicians you've got under your belt. You led me to believe –'

A firework goes off. It's like a light going on over my head. *You led me to believe*, I said … Like Rube always said, *Magicians get you to look in one direction when you should be looking in another.* I was *led* to believe. Like it says in the law of the convergence of unrelated phenomena, everything's connected. The early fireworks burst into life around us.

'You shouldn't have trusted me,' Ariadne says. 'What do you want to know?'

'Everything. And fast. There isn't a much time.'

'Once it was easy but now –' A bursting anemone turns Ariadne's face green. 'Economies can't expand forever, the money has to come from somewhere. Once it was taxes – when a king needed money he'd just dream up a new tax. It's no different now. The only ones who don't pay tax are crooks, the very wealthy and the churches.'

'So you don't pay taxes?'

'Hardly any.'

'What do you do in return?'

'We pay politicians.'

'Is there anything else? From either side?'

'Yes – silence. We indulge each other and then look the other way afterwards.'

'It looks like you can't look the other way any longer.'

Ariadne shakes her head and when she speaks

her voice is a whisper. 'No, I suppose I can't ...'
Fireworks have taken over the world.

The first shot has the three of us sniffing the asphalt
and the second shot has me going for my gat.
Beside me, Tsunami's crouched behind a car, while
in front, Ariadne's lying on the ground as still as
death. Around us is the sound of stockaded animals
milling towards the abattoir. There's a third shot
and I scan the surrounding buildings to see they're
coming from.
    'Don't move, Ariadne!' I say.
    'But a stone's sticking in my back!'
    'Be grateful you're alive to feel it.'
    I've worked it out: the shots came from our left
and the weapon was big, in the order of a .45. I look
for a gunman but all I can see are more fireworks,
courtesy of a bunch of kids who came by their
crackers courtesy of the internet. I haul Ariadne to
her feet. Tsunami never stopped standing.
    'It's only kids with a bunch of bungers.'
    Ariadne tries to dust herself off but Gucci doesn't
clean good. 'Where was I? That's right, I discovered
that politicians, far from being cornerstones of our
society, are very often the whackos of the world.
Most of the ones I dealt with took my money and
crept off into the night, hoping I wouldn't ask any
favours in return.'
    'But you did?'
    'Of course I did. That's the way it works, Rainbow.

You give people money and in return they do you favours – development approvals I didn't deserve, licences I shouldn't have got, contracts that should never have been signed. Politicians are the grease that enables the wheels of industry to turn without squeaking.'

'What about your research people – this Watchdog committee? What did they find that they shouldn't have?'

It's a long time before Ariadne answers and in that time the little family beside us – mother, father, daughter, dog – finish their picnic and, like the good citizens they are, clean up afterwards and place their rubbish in the receptacles provided. A lifetime passes – my lifetime, Ariadne's, Tsunami's, Imogene's.

I try to keep my voice calm as I repeat the question. 'What did they find that they shouldn't have?'

Ariadne shakes her head. Maybe it's the fumes. Maybe she's just trying to breathe.

Chapter 37

PAWNS

'Elected representatives think they're all-powerful when they're nothing of the kind – members of parliament are no more than egocentric mouthpieces. The real power's in the people who put them there. And by that I don't mean political parties. Parties are made up of envelope stuffers, old women who make lamingtons, volunteers who man booths at election time and ambitious people who want to get into parliament. But they're nothing but pawns.

'The real motive force of political parties is the extremists. They're the ones with the enthusiasm, the drive to keep the Bib-and-Bub parties going. They might be *extreme* socialists, *extreme* capitalists, *extreme* environmentalists, *extreme* anything. Whatever they are, they'll do pretty well anything to achieve their ends. They're the real terrorists.'

I cut across her. 'What did Watchdog find out? And make it snappy, Ariadne – if there wasn't much time before, there's even less now.'

The early fireworks have been and gone and the world's reclaimed by darkness.

'As with all political parties, the one in power now is both informed and propelled by a cabal. All cabals have an agenda. And on the agenda of the cabal of the party in power now is increased defence, less social services, reduced business tax, denial of global warming, no asylum seekers – and hardline religious intolerance. Except they don't call it that.'

'What *do* they call it?'

'Counter-terrorism.'

At the Strangefellows' Hall I lip-read the Mephistopheles joker saying: *To quote the master, you should know how to do evil if necessary.* The quote's from one of the works Rube made me study – *The Prince*, by Machiavelli: the *master* that Mephistopheles was quoting. Another way of saying that *the end justifies the means* – even if those means are as warped as the philosophy behind it.

'So their aim's to make people fear terrorism even more than they do now – be so fearful, in fact, that they'll accept *repression* in the name of security?'

Ariadne nods. 'That's only aim number one. Aim number two is to link terrorism to religion – as in: *some dogs bite, therefore all dogs bite.* And the third is to commit an act so shocking it will result in the banning of that religion.' She sees my look. 'Yes, they're *that* mad.'

'*Who*, Ariadne?'

'You already know the answer to that, don't you?' The night's revving up again; there's so much racket I'm back to lip-reading. 'Your Aunt Rube knew – her name came up on their radar early, which is why I wasn't surprised by her death. As I said, it's the nature of extremists that they'll go to any lengths to achieve their ends.'

She knows and yet she doesn't know; she's got nothing to do with what's happening and she's got everything to do with it; she's being loyal to someone she shouldn't be.

'They killed Rube.' I force myself to say it. 'And Harry and Queen. Then they went after Rory and were about to –' I stare at Ariadne. 'What did you do with Imogene? Was your phone call to the Minister a sham? Is my daughter safe?'

'As safe as she can be – considering.' Ariadne shrugs in the half light. 'They had the power to kill your Aunt Rube as well as the wherewithal to get away with it. Her death was part of a plan – all the deaths were. They could get rid of someone they needed to be rid of and blame it on terrorism.'

'It's Parkinson, isn't it? The real terrorist isn't some Middle Eastern bogey at all but a nice little Westerner called Parkinson. Who I had trouble recognising when I saw him because he was a big boy who became a small adult.'

'It's not as simple as that. Parkinson's only a foil. Didn't you tell me Harry said we were all terrorists? It's the system that's at fault. The system that our headmaster Mr Hercule and little Irving Morris are an integral part of. Under Nazism, no-one was guilty of any atrocities. Refugee children die but we don't kill them. Instead, we leave it to the workers in the abattoir. We see nothing, are responsible for nothing.' Her voice falters. 'It's the system.'

'What's he going to do now, this innocent foil of yours? What did your people discover?'

'It's like karma, the fate I brought on myself.'

It's confession time. 'All those years ago when you imagined I was on your side I was really on Parkinson's. Remember the time you thought you were rescuing me? Well, you weren't at all – I was just bait. Tom – Parkinson – was clever, devious, if you like. He wanted to get you. There were other times you've probably forgotten.' I haven't forgotten. 'The only time I stepped in to stop them was when they were about to hang you.'

'At least you were on my side then.'

Ariadne shakes her head sadly. 'When I realised you might die, I was afraid I'd get into trouble. You could have been hung.'

'Hanged.' The correction's automatic. 'You mean you knew what they were going to do?'

She shrugs. 'They told me. I was their friend and yours, playing both sides against the middle. While all the time I was … just as I'm doing now, right up until –'

Rube was keeping tabs on Parkinson when she stumbled on what they were up to and decided to monitor them.

Meanwhile, the MC's speaking, his voice echoing over the Harbour.

Up until now we've kept the nature of tonight's 'reveal' a close secret. Well, now I'm going to tell you what that 'reveal' is to be. But not right away. Let's have a physics lesson first, shall we? Do we want a little physics lesson? Louder, I can't hear you. Do we want a lesson in physics to justify our being called the Clever Country?

It's what they call a warm-up on this dull, lustreless night under a heavy cloud of suspicion.

With our beautiful Harbour as the backdrop we are about to see a sound-and-light show. But first, what are the colours of the spectrum? Murmurs issue from the crowd. *Come on, you can do better than that — you'd better because the eyes of the world are upon us. The first colour, on the count of three, is — one, two … Red!*

Hey, that's really good! Now on the count of three, the second colour — one, two … Orange!

The announcer's spinning the thing out, giving me a chance to put two and two together. I turn to Ariadne, this familiar yet unfamiliar person I used to know who's reappeared as a stranger. We've forced our way through the crowd till we're near the south-east pylon and the acrid fumes from the early fireworks linger in my nostrils and sit on my tongue. Beyond us the all-trusting, all-unsuspecting spectators go on with their chanting.

Yellow!

Chapter 38

COUNTDOWN TO TERROR

Louder, cries the MC, like Penelope unplucking her cloth as Ulysses draws close to home. *I want you to wake the gods.* After a bit more of this, it's time for *I Still Call Australia Home*, *We are the Ones* and *You are the Wind Beneath my Wings* – like we're about to go to war on a heaving wave of patriotism.

Ariadne raises her voice to be heard or maybe she's just raising her voice. Suddenly she looks agitated. Maybe it's the music; or maybe at long last it's the truth. 'I was alerted to a plot. Remember these people's minds work differently from yours and mine. First, they're mad which gives them the kind of power we could never possess. Second, they have political protection. And third, they have a Machiavellian turn of mind that would take your breath away.'

The music stops and it's time for the announcer again. *Remember this is beaming worldwide, people ... millions upon millions are watching, which means we've got an audience to die for. So let's knock 'em dead, shall we? It's practice time again, so let's do our rehearsal. On the count of three in this rainbow nation of ours, the first colour is …*

'I didn't go to the police because I – I was scared I'd be tarred with the same brush as the people we were monitoring. They'd think I was part of the plot. For the same reason, I couldn't go to the media. So I convinced myself that it – it couldn't happen here.'

'That *what* couldn't happen here?'

The Bridge looms above us, stilled of traffic. From where we're standing I can just make out the electric wires strung between the girders they'll use to set off the fireworks.

Ariadne's voice goes quiet. 'In a way I suppose I was part of it.' Under the hubbub I'm having trouble hearing her. 'The anti-terrorism people realised something big was planned but they didn't know what they were looking for.'

'And what *should* they be looking for?'

'I'm not – please believe I was never part of it. That is, I knew what they were planning but didn't think anything would happen – I thought it was all talk.'

Up till now, Tsunami's been silent, like she's been monitoring us, a black shadow among a lot of other black shadows – lithe and deadly beautiful. 'We're running out of time,' she says. 'From what I've heard, whatever *it* is will happen tonight. We have to cut to the chase.'

I turn to Ariadne. 'It's the Bridge at midnight, isn't it?'

'I promise, I didn't think …'

'Then for God's sake, Ariadne, think now!'

'It's meant to be a symbolic act, the destruction of a cultural icon. There are to be three linked explosions.'

'Why three?'

All right everyone, pay attention – the next colour, on the count of three, is … one, two …

'Why three?' I repeat.

Tsunami steps between us. She's the bomb expert, been here before, knows how it works.

'Anyone who's seen those old photos of the Bridge will know that an explosive device – even a pretty big one – would still leave the structure standing. There'd be some twisting but the Bridge was built to last and there'd be a strong chance it could be put together again, because each end's a self-supporting cantilever. I don't think they'd want anything to remain standing because it would water down the symbolism.' Tsunami says more because she knows more, after which I turn to Ariadne. 'So where are they – where have they put the bombs?'

Ariadne shakes her head, all the strength drained out of her. 'It's complicated. But basically, left, right and centre, linked by the same electrical wires they're using for the fireworks.'

'Do they want deaths or do they just want to destroy an icon?' I say.

The silence is broken by the roar of the crowd: *Blue!*

'Our information is they wanted to *maximise deaths*. They said it was for the greater good.' Ariadne pauses. 'Extremists don't like half measures.'

'Where's the primary bomb and how will it be detonated?'

Indigo!

The word sparks something in me, the way a detonator sets off a bomb. It's the word Rube uttered

just before she died. That was why they killed her –
because she knew. She worked out the significance
of what she'd discovered and was on the cusp of
stopping them when she was murdered, her death
made to look like the work of terrorists. She might
not have known the *how, when* and *where* but she
was well on the way to finding out when they killed
her.

'As I said before, everything was on a need to
know basis,' Ariadne goes on. 'There were cells and,
while my spies were privy to some, they weren't to
others. It's just become clear to me now.'

'Okay, how's the main bomb to be detonated?'

'They debated electric, electronic and impact
but finally decided on impact. There was mention
of *fulminate of mercury, chlorate of potash* and
something called *tetryl.*' Tsunami's nodding,
recognising detonators' constituents, what we're up
against. 'There's a sort of "baby bump" on top of the
bomb. According to our sources, the ones I didn't
fully believe, they rehearsed. They used a chock
of hardwood –' She points to Rube's box '– about
the size of that. They lodged it next to the button
to prevent the detonation. But that was rehearsal –
there'll be no block of wood tonight. The impact
will set off the bomb which will set off the other two
bombs.'

Something – a noise, movement – makes me spin
around. At first I think it's Pandora but it's only
Tsunami, no longer afraid of being too close.

'You're saying a block of wood stopped it going
off?'

Ariadne nods.

'Tom described it as "fail-safe". The bomb's impervious to impact from other directions – it had to be, he said, because he was working with amateurs. And, yes, a mere block of wood is enough to stop the detonator setting off the bomb.'

Chapter 39

SOMEWHERE PANDORA

'And where is it now – the bomb?'

The MC has led the crowd to the end of the spectrum, the dutiful audience has given the required responses and now he's speaking in the kind of voice used by Sunday school teachers explaining a Biblical passage – all-knowing, patronising and wrong.

Superimposed upon the Bridge will be an outline of our great country. One by one, we'll display each of the colours of the spectrum to symbolise who and what we are – starting with red and ending with violet. It will be a spectacular the like of which has never been seen before. Remember this show is being beamed live by satellite across the world and viewed by tens, maybe hundreds of millions of viewers – so make sure your noses are clean.

His captive audience laughs; Ariadne still hasn't replied.

'Where is it?' I repeat.

'At one of the meetings – Watchdog was able to record most of them – Tom made what he regarded as a joke. He said: *We don't want to blow this.*' Ariadne pauses, gathering her thoughts. 'Pyrotechnics are complex. It's not merely the effect, it's the practicality of realising that effect. A display has to be designed, co-ordinated – and safe. Installations are checked and double-checked – the security tonight is stringent.'

'Then how, where –?'

'Remember these people are in power, they're in charge. They control vital sections of our security organisations. They're here tonight in force. I remember a report saying they'll use those electronic bracelets they put on criminals, so that their central control knows where everyone is.'

The music starts again only this time it's not *Waltzing Matilda* or *Advance Australia Fair* or even *I Still Call Australia Home* but Hector Berlioz's *Symphony Fantastique* – the mad bit where the man kills his lover because he no longer trusts her. The crowd settles. They feel secure. In their midst are security people, wired up and ready to act. Somewhere, too, is Pandora.

There's only a short burst of the Berlioz but it's enough, like the organisers decided too much culture can kill. It's replaced by the shanty song about a convict leaving old England forever and coming to Botany Bay. The madman behind the planned deaths of so many must have chosen the music.

'Don't hurt him, will you?'

'He deserves to be hurt.'

'I'm not talking about Parkinson, I'm talking about our son. He's only helping because he's obedient. And obedience is a fine quality.'

I remember the stretch marks. When they met, Parkinson already had a son who became the *bearded* Parkinson. But there was another, younger, child who must be *their* son – Ariadne's and Parkinson's – fathered by Parkinson before Ariadne married her billionaire. So Parkinson has that much of a hold over her.

'You were someone Tom could never be and he hated you for it. When your Aunt Rube took you out of school he more or less shifted his campaign onto her. But it was a casual, desultory sort of business and it only became serious when Rube discovered Tom's other activities – his right wing, not "think-tank", but "act-tank". In his drive to frame an entire people, Tom wanted to what he called *neutralise* both you and your aunt. And I knew because we kept in touch, both on a personal level and through our respective groups. Watchdog fed his act-tank and vice-versa. But I didn't want you killed, Rainbow. Getting you to investigate terrorism was my idea; it meant I could keep tabs on you …'

Her voice fades as it's overtaken by the noise around us. I'd already worked out most of it.

'Parkinson grew up,' Ariadne goes on. 'At least he became an adult. Although he was a big boy he became a small adult, which was why you didn't recognise him. And he got to do what he liked doing best – hurting, even killing, people – at the same time as he was framing terrorists and, through them, adherents of their religion.

'He left clues at the scenes of his thugs' crimes to incriminate terrorists. It was my department that told him terrorists ritually cleansed themselves before killing, doing such things as dousing themselves with eau-de-cologne before setting out to commit their atrocities. Then there were the slogans …'

I butt in. 'And Babychino, Denise, or whatever her name was. She is – was – Parkinson's squeeze, isn't she? I caught her going through Harry's apartment and she came up with some cock-and-bull story about being Harry's girlfriend. It was easy for her to get personal details – Parkinson's group must have "ins" everywhere: the cops, security, the morgue. It was Parkinson's bad luck that Babychino was a lousy actor. Where's the bomb, Ariadne?'

Her hands drop helplessly by her sides. 'On the barge under the Bridge. They'll hoist the main bomb into place at the last moment. No-one will notice – it'll just be another black object against the night sky, part of the scenery. My son will be there …'

'Describe him.'

Ariadne describes Bertie Thomas, the kid I met on Camellia Pier all those aeons ago, the one with the story I didn't believe about being set upon by a gang of toughs and later being approached by terrorists.

'And Parkinson – where's he?'

'On the barge. Rainbow, I don't have to tell you of Tom's – predilections. He's got the death wish that all sadists have. I think he wants to die a martyr to his cause. Ironic, isn't it? That makes him just like them.' She reaches out and clutches my arm. 'Please don't hurt Bertie.'

I remove her hand from my sleeve and step away. 'Sorry, Princess, but no promises.'

They've blocked the approaches to the Bridge but it's too late to take that route even if I wanted to. I can't alert anyone because they'd arrest me on suspicion of whatever they want to be suspicious of when confronted by someone that doesn't exist. A guard with a walkie-talkie is patrolling the foot of the pylon. Beyond him I can make out the outline of a dinghy to be used in an emergency. This is an emergency.

I could cut and run, in which case I'd be safe. But it would also mean hundreds – maybe thousands – of innocent people would suffer. What kind of detonation will it be? *Impact*, Ariadne said, but that's just her information and the information could be wrong. How big is the bomb? *As big as a length of thread. Wrong analogy*, I reply. Then, giving her Rube's box and telling her to stay where she is, I make for the guards, taking Tsunami with me.

Security thrives on patterns and hugging the cold stone of the Bridge pylon we watch for this one. As my guard gets to the end of his patch – the pathway that bisects the park – light sparkles off his belt, his gun, the badge on his cap and his nightstick. He's not trying to hide because he wants to be seen – it adds to the sense of security of anyone watching. That's how I recognise him. It's also how I notice his companion.

I nod to Tsunami.

Chapter 40

ONE MINUTE TO MIDNIGHT

We're close enough to see the other guard and hear the contact words: *All quiet on the Western front?* Followed by the other guard's reply, delivered in a squeaky falsetto: *All quiet.*

Do not deviate from the script, warns the *Secur-A-Guard* booklet. *Safety lies in following the format to the letter – deviating will only compromise.* It's a short sequence because high security needs short sequences – it's no good discovering trouble half an hour after it occurs. In less than five minutes, the guard's back. Only this time I'm the guard – complete with cap, gun, nightstick and the right intonation – asking: *All quiet on the Western front?*

To which the response comes: *All quiet. What about you?*

My reply's already in my throat – *You're not supposed to say that* – when I remember the words of Thomas Jefferson, quoting someone else: *The price of liberty is eternal vigilance.* The other guard isn't the other guard because they've taken out the other guard just as they've taken out the rest of the security team. Which means the tall, thin man with the non-squeaky voice is not only the wrong man, he's also got orders to neutralise me.

Always get in first. Which is what Tsunami does because she's noticed him, too. He's a looming shadow with a job to do, only Tsunami does it better. He leaps in the air from a standing position because he knows his karate – correction, *tae kwon do.* I hear him say: *Metsuke no ezan – I'm gazing at the far mountains but can still see everything close at hand* as he comes at me in a flying side-kick. These boys play by the rules and he's not ready for Tsunami. Tsunami doesn't do rules. We find Ariadne still clutching Rube's box and make for the dinghy. More shadows, among them Pandora. I feel her presence, *sense* it with a terrible certainty. There's only one reality as I disable the second guard, unmoor the runabout, nod Tsunami aboard, load Rube's box in with her then – leaving the outboard motor up out of the water – tell Ariadne to use her rowing skills to get us out into the silver sea. At any moment a spotlight could slice across us. But right now we're a dark shape on darker water, moving silently.

It's three hundred metres from where we pushed out from Miller's Point to the Bridge's centre. The music's changed to something more up tempo because the organisers want to heighten the audience's expectations. There are hundreds of boats, the MC says, but only official ones are allowed under the Bridge. They don't want breaches of security getting in the way of festivities. Ariadne keeps rowing.

Only five minutes to go, folks. It's time to cast your minds back — at the same time remembering the traditional owners of this land — to that magical moment when Captain Arthur Phillip, our first governor, arrived at this historic site on this day in 1788 and declared it a colony in the name of His Royal Majesty, King George the Third. It's hard to believe, isn't it, that it all happened just a little over two hundred years ago. Harder still to imagine that not all that long ago the Bridge was no more than an idea in the mind of a man called Bradfield. It's like it's been here forever, one of life's immutables.

The world's reduced to the plash of oars in darkness, phosphorescence marking their tips before turing into flying fish, and our progress is that of a pregnant snail. The barge looms while the Bridge cuts a swathe through the stars. The barge is almost on us. So is midnight.

Only three minutes left, folks.

There's a lot of activity on the barge and the sound of raised voices carries down to us. Black figures scurry along the deck. It's only when we're almost upon them that I see the hook.

Two minutes.

It's dangling from a rope the same colour as the night sky, passed through a simple, manually operated block and tackle — a fiddle-block with two sheaves, one beneath the other — to ensure sufficient purchase. They can't use a motor for the same reason we can't use the outboard — there'd be too much noise. Everyone's meant to believe the bomb's part of the display, another rare device to be hauled into place at the last minute, the spotlights turned off to maintain the magic.

Speaking of the traditional owners, I'm sure you've all heard of the Rainbow Serpent. While we're celebrating the coming of the white man, we must also acknowledge the inherent belief of the Aborigines. Or should I say the Koori *people. According to the Kooris, the Rainbow Serpent is where it all began …*

One minute to midnight.

I grip one ratline while Tsunami grabs another then draw the gat I took from the guard and hand it to Ariadne. Apart from the knife, I'm now weaponless, but where we're headed, the weight of a gun could be the difference between waking up tomorrow and dying.

'Two things, Princess. Hang onto this – you might need it. And with the other hand keep hold of the barge.' I turn to the figure in black poised beside me. 'Ready?'

Tsunami nods.

Five figures are hauling on the rope and they're all going to die, except they don't know it because it's a detail they haven't been made privy to. There's no other way it can work – they've got to get the bomb into place and they know too much to be allowed to live. Only two are meant to survive – Parkinson and his kid; the two are wearing lightweight divers' outfits while the rest … The rope dangling from the Bridge is five-eighths abaca – good, strong stuff also known as Manila hemp – and it's hanging from the block and tackle under the platform below the Bridge forty-seven metres above our heads. The bomb's a giant Rubik's cube covered with plastic and innocent-looking – except for the giveaway bump at the top.

Forcing my eyes to adapt – *gazing at the far mountains while seeing everything close at hand* – I can just make out the steel baffle jutting from the platform designed to make contact with the lump on the cube. The men will have been instructed to haul extra hard at the end to ensure the impact-detonation occurs, although they won't know that's the reason. They'll have been told something else.

I work my way up the side of the hull, aware of Tsunami beside me. The barge is black and cold but it's a lot worse where we're headed. The MC's begun his countdown. I ease myself over the rusty railing. Tsunami follows.

I hear Parkinson's last-minute instructions. 'We're hauling up a fireworks display and it *must* hit right on the button when the man says *indigo*. So that you remember, the sequence goes *red, orange, yellow, green, blue, indigo, violet* – got it? The timing's sixty seconds from go to whoa – from when the man says *red* to when he says *indigo*. The Bridge will light up with the relevant colour when the MC names it but don't be distracted. There'll be two seconds a haul and there are thirty hauls, just like in a tug of war.'

'What happens when the bundle hits the Bridge?'

'Like I've told you a million times, there'll be a surprise fireworks display spelling out the words: *SPARED BY ALLAH!*'

'All this for a sign?'

'Remember that we're not the crazies around here. We don't believe in death – we're far more civilised than that. We're just making a statement. And that statement is that thousands of innocent people could have died tonight. We want to make people afraid, make them sit up and take notice, allow the counter-terrorism people to finally take the appropriate action.' He pauses; he's said enough. 'Bertie will do the call. Heave!'

We could try to take them now but we'd never succeed. There's too many. The men are leaning into their task as I come around the side of the wheelhouse, five shapes bent low, grunting, and their words drift across to me like hammer blows.

> *I must down to the sea again,*
> *to the lonely sea and the sky,*
> *And all I ask is a tall ship*
> *and a star to steer her by,*
> *And the wheel's kick and the wind's song*
> *and the white sail's shaking*
> *And a grey mist on the sea's face*
> *and a grey dawn breaking.*

The words seem at odds with what they're doing until I realise it's the sailor's old-style drill to get the rope-haulers working in synch – sixty seconds they've got and sixty seconds is what the poem will give them. They're up to *sky* and me and Tsunami are on the opposite side to the men as the chain attached to the rope rattles around the capstan. The bundle lurches into the air and we creep aboard as Bertie, the boy in the long socks, says, 'Remember, two seconds a haul, right on the button, no more, no less – the secret's in the rhythm. *Haul!*'

Chapter 41

RUBE'S BOX

The men chant and the chain rattles around the capstan as I make my way up the side of the bomb. All the while Rube's words are hammering through my cerebellum: *Do you remember how to defuse bombs, Rainbow? It depends, Rube. It depends whether I've got all the time in the world or a matter of seconds; it depends whether I'm on the ground or swinging from a rope hundreds of feet in the air and making a rapid, jerky ascent; and most important of all, it depends if the bomb's detonated electronically and not through impact at all.*

The plastic tears under my weight, forcing me to scrabble for a new hold. The crowd's roaring *orange* and the men are chanting *by* as I abseil into space before slamming back hard against the load. The bundle's three metres by three metres and about the same height, but a lot of it's soft packaging behind a ribbed framework of steel bars. I manage to grab one of the bars just as the plastic gives way, hauling myself in again. Tsunami's beside me.

Yellow! yells the crowd.

Kick! bellow the men on the barge.

The Bridge will collapse inwards, 50,000 tonnes of steel crumpling as its weight bears the structure down. The men on the barge will be killed when the bomb goes off, followed by those in the nearest pleasure craft as the wave gets going. But I won't be around to see it because I've got fifteen seconds left – twenty at best – and there's no time for a cheerio call or to work out where I went wrong or how things might have been different. I've got to focus on the detonator – how it works, how to get to it, how to defuse it.

Far below I can make out the movement in the crowd as the security people start their surge towards the Bridge. They've finally noticed what's happening and it's confirmed their worst fears. To the north and south searchlights swing towards us then suddenly go out.

The load's swinging like a pendulum in a coffin clock as we draw close while I'm tearing at the plastic like a boy with a Christmas present to see what's underneath. When I needed it, the plastic tore; now, when I don't, it resists to the end; I pull out the knife I took from the gunman in the brothel and start cutting. No-one on the barge has noticed us – they're too intent on their task. Placing the knife between my teeth, I continue climbing.

I'm looking for the button designed to hit the platform under the Bridge and send the Harbour Bridge sky-high; a button and a bunch of wires. I'm also looking for the fail-safe, the standby device they always install in case the impact detonation fails. It's the first thing a defuser looks for – the fallback, the second detonator, the pointer being the aerial saying it's electronic or a blinking red light which says there's a timing mechanism. Tsunami scrabbles alongside me, black and shiny as a shark, her eyes following my every movement.

Blue!

I feel like a suicide on a ledge with the crowd chanting *Jump!* Out of nowhere Parkinson appears. That's the thing about mad people, they can be relied upon to do mad things. *Why didn't you stay with him*, I asked Ariadne. *Because he's mad. I love him but he's mad. It didn't stop me loving him and doing what he told me to do but I could never have married him.* Besides, he had a wife who *could* put up with his madness.

He's discarded his oxygen pack, mask and goggles, he's swung himself onto the bomb and he's gaining on us. I wonder what death will be like, whether it comes complete with a kaleidoscope of colour or just blackness, a slow clawing at consciousness as my brains scatter. The impact ledge is closing in and with the shortening of the cable, the load has momentarily stopped. I hold my breath. The men below will shout *and a grey dawn breaking* and the bomb will hit the impact hammer and that will be the end of everything.

Faintly through the midnight air I hear – or think I hear – someone, somewhere, intoning the word *indigo* just as the men bellow *breaking* and suddenly he's upon me, my torturer of old, Parkinson, only now he's no longer twice my size but smaller and he hasn't got a lot of bully boys to help him. I'm the one with the upper hand but a lot of good it'll do me. The uprush of the word that will mean the final haul on the rope that will depress the plunger and detonate the explosive is rising in the throats of the men on the barge like the suction preceding the formation of a tidal wave.

Parkinson has the strength that comes with madness, the desperation of a man who believes in something strongly enough to die for it. I'm not going to succeed while he's all-powerful because that's what he's always been. He's a fanatic, an extremist, and this is his extreme mission. His hands grapple at my throat as the Bridge's underbelly looms. Around us strands of wires connect the fireworks to the glinting packages of installations. The bomb looks benign by comparison – safe, almost comforting.

I find his pressure points without thinking. I'm in the playground again but now I've got my torturer at my mercy. The load is surging upwards, taking me with it, and we're on the upward stroke of the hammer blow. Suddenly, I'm an animal acting on instinct. And my instinct is to raise Parkinson above my head and lodge him in the rapidly narrowing crevice between Bridge and bomb, ensuring he's out of the way of the detonator button but just to one side, a human buffer to prevent detonation as the crowd screams *Indigo!* and the crew on the barge separate the last word of their chant into *brea-* and then *-king!* and I hear the sound as a body crunches and wait for the explosion that says I've failed, that tells me instinct isn't enough, was never going be enough, even as I swipe the knife across the ropes in a final desperate attempt to stop the world exploding.

White air, silence. A figure grows wings and takes to the sky, hurtling into space. As the men below roar *-king* I imagine I see Tsunami smiling. Only I can't see Tsunami. Then comes the crunch. I look away.

There's no explosion.

As the fireworks go off, I feel like I'm suspended in space, the flat, black Harbour below me, the crowd a collection of broken rocks and the spotlights smoking ruins. Water, when you hit it after a fall from this height is as hard as diamond, and that's what I'm falling towards. The bomb has swung around until it's above me. I grapple to turn it and my hands find wires. I clutch at them and they come away. I wait for the explosion but it doesn't occur. Too late, I try to force the bomb under me. It must be too late – falling this far at an acceleration rate of thirty-two feet per second per second I'll hit the water and the bomb will land on top of me and afterwards my body will be borne down to the smoky depths of the Harbour. *Think like an animal. On second thoughts, don't think at all. Just act.*

I give one final, desperate heave as the water rushes to meet me.

There's no splash, not even the hint of one. Just, close at hand, the suspiration of splintering wood, the noise of exploding fireworks, multi-coloured lights shooting into the sky and breaking into flowering petals and fountains of light. And, far away, the faint roar of the crowd. I must have blacked out. Because when I can see again, I've surfaced, alive enough to make out an anxious face peering over the edge of the dinghy.

'Are you all right, Rainbow?'

I blink up. 'I've just fallen into the Harbour from the top of what must be the equivalent of a fifteen-storey building ...'

'Where's my son? Where's that woman? And where's Tom?'

I tell her I don't know times three as her hands grapple for me. She helps me aboard and immediately I hear the rattle of a motor starting.

'The bomb landed on the barge and you landed on the bomb and the bomb didn't explode because it was the right way up. The people on the barge must all have died but I didn't see the others who were on the bomb with you – that woman and Tom ...' There are tears in her voice but then Ariadne's all business. 'Lie down so you can't be seen.'

Boats are coming our way. There'll be police and security people, including, inevitably, anti-terrorism squads. I lie as still as I can next to Aunt Rube's box.

'Don't give anyone reason to suspect there's anyone in the boat apart from you,' I murmur.

'There isn't.'

IF YOU ENJOYED THIS INSTALMENT
OF MISTER RAINBOW, BE SURE
TO CHECK OUT THE OTHER
BOOKS IN THE SERIES.

978-1-922057-20-4 (digital)
978-1-922057-45-7 (print)
Winner of silver in the 2012 Independent Publishers Awards.
She's a surgeon, she's beautiful and she desperately wants
Mister Rainbow to shed some light on her husband's past.
But when he does, she wishes he hadn't. Because what
Rainbow discovers is a handless hood – and a
whole lot of murders.
Rainbow's a retro private eye who keeps himself to himself.
He lives (illegally) on a boat in Sydney Harbour, has no
identity, and frequents speakeasies. He's also got a
nemesis called Pandora …
The Case of the Hood With No Hands is the first novel in the
sensational Mister Rainbow heptalogy.

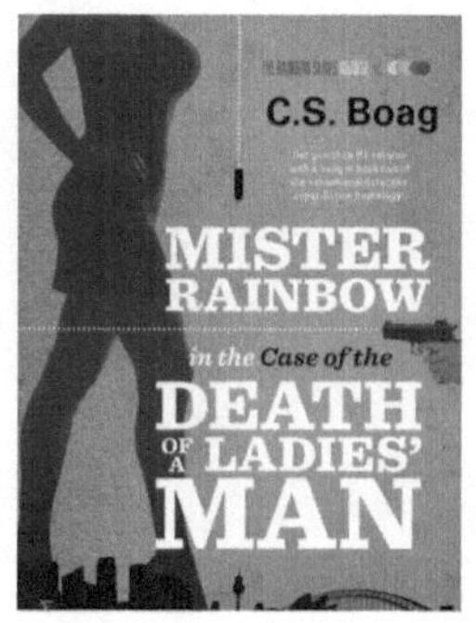

978-1-922057-53-2 (digital)
978-1-922057-54-9 (print)
When Mister Rainbow finds a headless honcho in a
Kings Cross alleyway, the tattoo around the corpse's neck
leaves little doubt as to its identity. Thomas L. Tycho was
everybody's enemy – a trickster, a dirty dealer, and a wide
boy who made the mistake of wide boys the world over – not
making himself narrower when the gun went off.
The killer's identity, however, proves more elusive – as
everybody hated Tommy, anybody could have popped him.
His wife, his girlfriend, and half of Sydney's underworld
all had motive, but Mister Rainbow smells something
fishier than usual, and it's got nothing to do with
what's floating in the harbour …
The Case of the Death of a Ladies' Man is the second novel in
the sensational Mister Rainbow heptalogy.

978-1-922057-75-4 (digital)
978-1-922057-76-1 (print)

A trip to Paris in the company of a beautiful
dame would be many men's idea of heaven. But a flight to
France with the gorgeous Helen Damnation rapidly
spirals into a journey to hell.
Rainbow's daughter is missing and he doesn't know who's
taken her – or why. Nor does he know where she might have
gone, until he enlists the help of a childhood mate – now a spy
– Ace Mollema. But can he trust the spook? Or the beautiful
dame, for that matter? Above all, can he save the kid?
Sparks fly when Rainbow assumes a temporary identity to
get a passport – and those sparks quickly turn to fire. Can
Rainbow rescue his daughter? And if he does, can he work out
the significance of the Bullets at the Ballet ...
The Case of the Bullets at the Ballet is the fourth novel in the
sensational Mister Rainbow heptalogy.

Also in the series

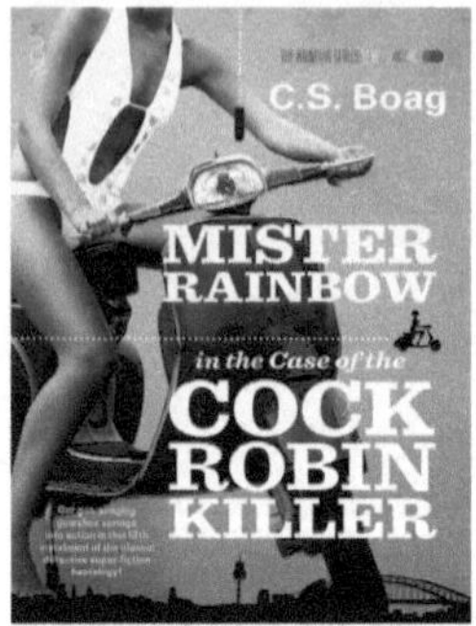

978-1-922057-89-1 (digital)
978-1-922057-88-4 (print)

Rainbow's got the blues. His girlfriend's dumped him; his
assassin mate Rory's found God; his Aunt Rube's as sick as a
bad joke; and his ex-wife's thrown up a barricade – all right, a
cordon bleu – around his daughter Imogene.
So when a snake's let loose in a laboratory, his ballet teacher's
under siege and a nasty little joker by the name of Cock Robin
cops it, Rainbow climbs into the ring because it's his job – but
also because he needs the distraction.
In the red corner he finds an unpredictable dame called
Tsunami; a crooked cop; a tough-as-granite developer;
a politician; a couple of thugs; a paparazzo; and
too many bodies.
While in the blue corner – yeah, that's Rainbow's – there's
just two dames in distress and a bald journo. The clue is blue.
But is that blue as in the moody blues, blue blood, a bad blue,
a stoush – or just plain old-fashioned blue murder?
The Case of the Cock Robin Killer is the fifth novel in the
sensational Mister Rainbow heptalogy.